COVEN HALL

HAYLE COVEN ENFORCER: ONE

PATTI LARSEN

This book was made real thanks to Dee, David, Dianne, Kirstin, Lisa, Katie, Matthew and all of my Hayle coven witches. Thank you for reading and loving this crazy family like I do.

Thanks, Kirstin!
ISBN-13: 978-1-998948-02-4

DEDICATION

For David, because magic *is* real.
And in loving memory of Dee.
So mote it be.

PROLOGUE

I went with Ethpeal to her room, not knowing what else to do. Her mother's decision to banish her eldest daughter wasn't a surprise, not really, though cutting her free from the family magic had to have hurt the young witch I loved.

If it had, Ethpeal didn't show it or react openly as she packed her bags with calm and the enduring confidence that I loved about her. Only a short time ago, she'd confronted her coven leader over Mahalia's newborn daughter, Belvah, and the damage she'd done to her second born in her selfishness and craving for power. The poor weak, sickly little thing would live, thanks to me and to Ethpeal, but it was clear to me the only remaining

Hayle child would be a mere shadow of her mother.

Exactly Mahalia's plan, I suppose.

I sat on the bed, soft whines escaping under my breath, tail swishing back and forth as I struggled for something to say. "She got her way," I whispered at last. "She's the only powerful one left. I should have done more, Ethpeal. I should have done something." I might not have had the power I used to, my demon magic gone when I was banished from Demonicon into this body, my silver Persian form abandoned in the streets of London over a century ago. If it hadn't been for Ethpeal's great-great grandmother, Thaddea Hayle, I wouldn't have survived. My lifetime spent protecting and guiding the witches of this coven felt like a waste, to have come to a tragic and terrible ending and I couldn't help but feel responsible for Ethpeal's predicament. Or Belvah's.

"Sass," Ethpeal turned to me at last, after her long silence, sighing deeply as she sank to the bed to stroke my fur. "It's all right, Sass."

"It's not." I hung my head, weeping. "I failed again, Thad," I whispered to the ghost of the girl I'd loved, the one who'd saved me, not just physically but who brought me back from the brink of giving in. I owed her and the Hayle family I guarded much more than they ever owed me. "I'm so sorry." There was no doubt in my mind that with Mahalia's decision to banish her eldest, powerful daughter that the line of Hayle witches would die out in the most tragic and terrible way possible.

And there was nothing I could do about it.

Ethpeal gathered me into her arms and held me close, humming softly, a tune I knew so very well, comforting me where I couldn't do the same for her as Thaddea reached through time and space to love me once again. "Dear Sassafras," Ethpeal said, "you've done more than any cat, any witch, could ever have done for this family." She sighed again. "And look how we've rewarded your loyalty and faithfulness."

I pressed my cheek to hers, paws on her shoulders. "Where will we go?" I suddenly didn't care, knowing it didn't matter as long as I was with her. But she shook her head, pulled me away, fixed me with her blue eyes—Hayle eyes so familiar to me—and a determined expression.

"We," she said, "aren't going anywhere."

"You must," I said. "She banished you."

"Yes." She kissed the top of my head gently. "But you, dear cat, must remain."

Rage wouldn't come. No arguments, no fight in

me at all. Not because I didn't want to go with her—I did, desperately. But because I knew what she was about to ask me to do, I couldn't even consider turning her down.

"Watch over my sister, I beg you," Ethpeal said. "As you have Hayle witches for so long. I'm sorry to ask you, Sass." Her hands stroked my fur endlessly as she spoke, power embracing me while mine hugged her back. "It won't be easy for you here, alone. Stay with Auntie Winnifreth and the ladies," she stood, grabbed a small bag, levitated the old-world trunk she'd packed with her things, "and out of Mahalia's sight. But do what you can to protect my sister."

"And you?" I shivered, alone on her quilt as her shadow fell over me. She might have been severed from the Hayle family magic, but there was nothing but power in Ethpeal Hayle. Not just Thaddea's either, but that of her grandmother, Auburdeen, that magic shared with her on purpose when she was still in her mother's womb. I'd done my best to protect her from Mahalia, not knowing my two beloved Hayle witches would have their own intent, echoes of themselves or not.

"And me." If I sensed even a moment of hesitation from Ethpeal, I would have abandoned her request and gone with her. But she seemed decided already, almost content, as though she'd made plans without my knowledge for just such a contingency. Perhaps the gift of her ancestresses would be enough. I could only hope. "I'm off to see who I really am."

With that, my darling Ethpeal, my heart and my charge, turned her back on the family that abandoned her in their cowardice and left me behind.

CHAPTER ONE

One never knows how life will unwind, though I'd always been of a mind to plan ahead. I blamed my dear Sassafras, mainly, for my foresight and deliberate intention. I must admit, the two powerful witches whose power I carried were hardly innocent, either, as much as they preferred to remain as autonomous as possible but in the periphery. Nor was I given to hysterics or bouts of emotional extravagance despite the fact one of those two witches was a temperamental redhead I knew had made her name being as impulsive as she was impressive. If I only carried my great-grandmother Auburdeen's echo with me, perhaps my rather stoic nature might have been challenged and made my life that much more uncomfortable. But knowing I also carried her mother, Thaddea, with that ancestor's steady and kindly nature smoothing her own daughter's edges, I felt I was left as much myself as could be expected under the circumstances, Fey father's bloodline and demon cat's magical interference notwithstanding.

The life of a Hayle witch was nothing if not complicated. Whether I was still a Hayle witch or not. Despite the fact Mahalia had chosen to banish me, both of the women who'd been leader once insisted I was more a Hayle than the one who bore me would ever be. Odd how I felt little difference despite the loss of the family magic. Yes, I missed its steady presence, but it was apparent to me Sassafras and his tampering had altered me sufficiently that instead of weakened by the loss of the coven's support, I felt, instead, somewhat buoyed, and nervously excited to discover what I could accomplish on my own.

"Chin up, Eth," I whispered to myself as I faced the wards between me and Harvard Yard. "Steady on."

What I hadn't intended was my reaction upon my arrival to my second choice in life. My first look at the brick buildings and towering oaks, elms, maples and other trees that made up the Boston campus brought tingling goosebumps I hadn't expected, despite my carefully laid decisions and the path I'd taken when the one I'd been born to was torn out from under me. Alternate choice or not, there was something imminently dominating and yet quietly comfortable about the space where I intended to spend the next three years—or more, who knew?—of my life.

The early September air carried a hint of coolness without being chill, warm sun overhead peeking through the bank of gray-edged clouds pushing their way across the city's skyline, slowly devouring the view above the towering walls of the Yard, damp scent and tingle threatening a storm brewing. I knew better than to blame my unease on the pending inclement weather. Others might be willing to look aside when faced with signs of truth, but I'd spent my life under another storm and learned if I didn't take full responsibility for my actions while examining the decisions and activities of those around me, I'd quickly fall prey to cowardice and an inability to act when action was of the greatest necessity.

Not that acting had done me a whit of good. I didn't sigh as I hefted the small carrier in my right hand, grip firm on the worn leather, the hefty trunk I'd inherited from my Auntie Winnifreth left behind for the moment at the small hotel where I'd spent the previous night. Such an expression of dissatisfaction would do nothing to amend the fact that I'd failed to protect my family from my mother.

Yes, that sat badly on my narrow shoulders, making me shrug somewhat despite the fact such weight was imagined and no one walking past me or in my vicinity could see the burden I bore. But I knew, how well did I know, just how badly I'd managed to make a mess of things by letting my temper—no blaming GrandMum Burdie for my reaction—get the better of me and put me in a position where Mahalia (I no longer called her Mother, not even to spite her) could finally act against me.

I tsked softly at myself once, allowing that moment of frustration, before shaking it off again. Spilled milk gone to waste, that effort. One week. I'd had only to wait one week, and I would have been eighteen, ready to challenge Mahalia Hayle to the coven's leadership. Success would have been within my grasp. Instead, here I stood, only four days older, but that intention dead and buried.

My pleated skirt ruffled along the hem as a breeze picked up, scattering a handful of leaves across the sidewalk just before the gate to my destination. It felt as though the stone walkways that segmented the Yard, stretching out into the campus, were a world away despite their proximity. Taking my own advice firmly in hand, I straightened my shoulders and raised my head, marching onward into the future.

I'd dressed rather carefully in a dark blue drop-waisted dress and polished navy Mary Jane's, my black waves precisely contained in a headband scarf, pearls that had been a gift from the aunties settled neatly on my collarbones. Though much more comfortable in trousers and soft shoes, I knew today of all days, appearances mattered.

Today, I applied to Coven Hall, the first Hayle—or not Hayle, not anymore—to do so, and I had every intention of making a confident impression.

My shoes clicked on the stone walk when I passed through the wards, drawing a deep breath of relief when they did nothing to restrain me. Yes, I feared some reaction to my arrival, though I admit as I allowed that brief respite from my anxiety, internally, for sure, something stirred that I wasn't expecting. It took every ounce of my strength to keep myself from stumbling, pausing instead to pretend to observe my surroundings as I caught my breath.

What was that feeling? It stirred beneath me, like a dark sigh, some kind of magic I didn't recognize and yet swelled, infinitely familiar despite myself. Something like a flower unfolded the barest amount, like a black blossom waking after a long slumber, and had me shivering from the effect. Burdie's sigh of contentment had me even more shaken, though comforted somewhat, as well. If she was happy, surely this was a good experience to have? Apparently, I had a great deal more to learn than I thought, and not just from the teachers here at Coven Hall.

What other wonders awaited me now that I was free of the family magic?

A few other students hurried past me, heads down, the storm clouds overhead bearing down like doom coming upon us. That got me moving again, my long strides uninhibited by the skirt, at least, the dress a last-minute addition thrust upon me by Auntie Belladonna.

"It makes you look so tall," she'd said when she slipped it in my bag, hurrying as my other aunt had hurried, both spinster Ambrose sisters weeping quietly as they helped me pack and escape before Mahalia could change her mind about banishing me and come to finish off her eldest daughter. No, I wouldn't have put that past my former coven leader, her mental state far from optimal the past five years. Mahalia's decision to strip the Hayle power from her own mother, Lilibeth, had come at a cost only a few of us knew about. That cost came at the expense of Mahalia's slowly deteriorating mental health as the power of the coven fought her every single moment of every single day. I'd taken that battle as a sign I'd be coven leader one day.

Thank goodness for best laid plans in duplicate.

"And the pearls." Auntie Hyacinth had dropped them into my case after the shoes they'd dug from my closet. "Dear Ethpeal, what will we do without you?"

The first raindrop fell as I strode up the steps into Widener Library and passed the front doors, turning to observe as a crack of thunder rolled through the Yard, splatter of wetness turning to a torrent that gushed over the stairs and spit temperamental moisture through the entry, pooling in shining puddles reflecting back the flicker of lightning that followed.

More thunder. I took it as a sign, hopefully a good one, though surely a storm was coming for me, too. I straightened and lifted my chin, carrying on into the foyer, turning toward the far-left side of the vaulted and imposing entry of the main library toward the whisper of magic luring me onward. I watched as two others passed through the plain wooden doorway before following without slowing my strides, case swinging at my side, passing through the wards and shielding without a hiccup and into Coven Hall beyond.

I did allow a sigh then, a small and relieved one. While the wards had allowed me entry at the gate, there had been no promise Coven Hall itself would permit my presence. There had been a moment I'd worried, allowed myself to crack, for anxiety to wake and whisper its concern that perhaps I wouldn't be able to pass. I was covenless, after all, no longer tied to a family, at least not officially. Perhaps the power of my ancestors gave me the wherewithal or, more likely, I'd been foolish to worry. And what role, I wondered as I carried on, did the dark blossom that had awoken on my arrival play, if any? Regardless of my questions and concerns, Coven Hall welcomed all with magic, it seemed, and my penchant to nerves was groundless.

With this new hurdle surmounted, I was ready for anything, allowing excitement to replace my previous fear. The moment I entered the dark-paneled and equally impressive entrance to Coven Hall, magic floating in the darkness above, stone floor beneath my feet sparking with power, I spotted a tall and towering woman in a black robe, blue piping around her face and down the front of her cloak. An Enforcer, and confirmation for me

I'd made the right choice. If only Mahalia knew it was her constant conflicts with other covens, her greed in recruiting heavily those who belonged to other families, enough she raised the concern of the North American Witches Council itself, that gave me the idea for my alternative plan. She'd have hated to know it was the sight of two such Enforcers, their powerful presence leaving an indomitable mark on my young mind when they'd appeared to chastise our family for stepping over legal lines, that led me here to Coven Hall and what I hoped would be my future.

Becoming an Enforcer seemed like a fairy tale back then. It was all I could think about now.

So, when it was my turn to step up to the desk in the middle of the dark hall with the filing line of young witches come to make their own marks upon the world, I was proud to nod to the hooded official looking up at me from the other side of the desk.

"Name?" She sounded tired and rather bored. Before she really looked at me, even as I spoke.

"Ethpeal Elizabette Hayle," I said.

I might as well have attacked her with magic, by the way she reacted. And I realized then and there, the storm I'd thought I'd dodged? Hadn't even begun.

CHAPTER TWO

From the pinched and unhappy expression that the witch wore shortly after her wide, hazel eyes and open-mouthed squeak alerted me to pending problems, my previous concerns were coming home to roost. Not that I intended to back down without a fight. My family's recent history, mainly due to my mother's terrible recruitment behavior and utter disregard for the sanctity of the North American Witches Council, had certainly created a level of worry I'd done my best to set aside until proved otherwise.

The proof, I now guessed, was right in front of me and about to blow up in my face.

A bit melodramatic, yes, I admit, and ultimately

inaccurate. That didn't keep the witch from turning to the other next to her, whispering something in haste, before leaping to her feet with her black velvet robe swishing, to circle the large, wooden desk and come to my side. She quickly ushered me out of the way of those waiting behind me, stares and curious looks only driving my shoulders back and my chin to further elevation. They would not see me cringe or bend under the pressure of this attention. Nor would they simply walk me out of here and abandon me on the streets of Boston without some kind of explanation.

"This way." She spun and hurried off without waiting to see if I'd follow and I admit to you now, I almost did not. But the sight of that same towering Enforcer watching me with a slowly growing frown on her face had me finally setting my path to pursue the rapidly departing witch who was disappearing down a long, wood-paneled corridor lined with heavy, carved doors. I spared sideways glances for a few of those portals, their surfaces etched with images that stirred my imagination, from flames to a field of flowers and even one with a hideous beast snarling its cruel intent from the depths of the polished wood. The corridor seemed to stretch on forever, magic drawing it out, though I noted the tingle of power as the witch turned just as a side hallway appeared out of nowhere and took control of my own path then, seeking out the lines of power that led me much more clearly than she could to the reason for this march to uncertainty.

I emerged at last through a doorway, the witch's hem swirling through a puddle of blue power just ahead of me, her short, quick strides no match for my long, steady ones. I was almost on her heels when I stepped through and had to hold myself back with a sharp intake of breath when I realized she'd come to a sudden halt.

The room I'd found myself in felt nothing like Coven Hall's magical confines, the towering ceiling overhead unclouded by darkness, crown moldings arching overhead. I took note of the oppressive appearance of the witches in the gold-framed portraits who lined the large room with their judgmental stares, feeling the touch of power from each of them, the hint of the person who they'd been, echoes lingering as though unwilling to leave. My shoes slid slightly on the polished wooden floor beneath me, light pouring in from the multitude of windows assuring me the storm had passed outside, though the one brewing in here was far from over.

In fact, it had just begun.

I had one moment to process this new location

while my guide spluttered something to the woman behind the desk at the far end of the room. I took note she made no effort to close the distance to the other witch who stood and slowly circled toward us, unable to stop my own power from sampling the nervousness that arose in my shivering guide as she bobbed a hasty curtsy before speaking.

"Ethpeal Hayle," she squeaked. Looked up at me with enough anxiety I was certain she expected something monstrous from me before she refocused on the other witch in the room. "Excuse me, Headmistress." She was gone without another word, brushing past me, through the doorway, closing it behind her with one final peek at me, those hazel eyes full of fear as she did.

I turned back to the witch who watched me, doing my best to suppress my own nerves. As part of my plan, I'd steeled myself for the very real possibility I'd be shunned from Coven Hall thanks to my mother, though I'd allowed myself the kind of hope that I really knew better than to harbor. Hope always led me to disappointment and, despite knowing how grim that outlook made me, I allowed myself to settle into that truth even as another door opened and two people hurried inside.

I was so surprised by their sudden appearance, I

felt my resolve slipping, though instead of the fear I'd seen in my previous encounter, the tall, slim man in the heavy blue and gold robe nodded to me with what seemed to be real kindness while his counterpart, a short, sturdy witch whose robe bore embroidered flowers in a multitude of shades so realistic it seemed she carried a garden with her, openly grinned at me before schooling her features.

"Professor Gilleland." The witch who watched me from the far end of the room had a low, dusty voice and an unkind face to match, dark eyes under straight, black hair severe and controlled, as her magic seemed to be. There was beauty in her I knew could shine through if she allowed it, but the wall of power she bore around her like a fortress wouldn't allow it to show through. Instead, she had the stern and uncompromising disdain of one who knew she held my fate in her hands and was not afraid to wield whatever choice she made like a weapon against me.

Against my mother, more than likely. If only Mahalia was here to bear the brunt of it instead of me.

"Headmistress Lund." The man spoke, obviously Gilleland, the woman beside him clenching her hands in front of her, gaze sliding back and forth between me and the Headmistress of Coven Hall, doing little to hide her nervous energy though he seemed calmly collected and even charismatic.

"Professor Carista." Lund's expression flattened further while the auburn-haired witch bobbed a nod in her direction, distracted by my presence enough to illicit irritation from her Headmistress. The head of Coven Hall didn't seem surprised by this visit, however, so she must have either summoned them or expected their intervention. "I'll be with you both shortly."

Ah. Unexpected. Understood.

"We're here to represent our newest applicant." Carista blurted those words without glancing my way. "Imagine our delight to discover, after all this time, a Hayle witch is applying to Coven Hall." This time she did look my way, flashing me another smile.

"Kate," Gilleland muttered softly with a shake of his head before speaking up, that smooth and polished tone returned. "My esteemed colleague and I would be delighted to offer our newest student guidance during her first days."

"Delighted." Kate Carista nodded quickly.

"You're both under certain assumptions, it seems." Headmistress Lund didn't move a fraction, holding still and cold despite her full stance in the beam of sunlight pouring in through the window behind her. It was almost as though she repelled even that warmth in her utter need to control her surroundings.

Professors Gilleland and Carista exchanged a look before returning their attention to the Headmistress.

"I beg your pardon," he said.

Lund finally moved, no longer a statue but eerily light on her feet and fluid. Was she fully human or did she boast some other paranormal lineage in her bloodline? Or perhaps she simply refused to allow even a modicum of humanity any sway over her. Whatever the case, when she did step out of the sunbeam and into the center of the room, her dark eyes settling on me again, I realized she was barely taller than the flowery professor and only seemed to loom thanks to her magic and rigidity of control. I had inches on her and fought the urge to bow my head to her, the pressure of her presence so dominant I instantly disliked her.

The feeling, apparently, was mutual.

"We have issues at hand," Lund said then, holding up her fingers and bending one down as she went on. "First, the Hayle family has never contributed to nor attended Coven Hall since their formation as a coven."

"Then it's about time, isn't it, for that to change." Professor Gilleland sounded reasonable enough, but I caught the faint thread of concern in his voice the way his eyes creased around the corners, handsome face calm but as careful as his tone had become. Clearly, he was accustomed to dealing with the Headmistress and was expecting some hammer to fall I had, as yet, to ascertain. "Wouldn't you say?"

"Were that the only issue, David," Lund said, stressing his first name as though using it, not out of familiarity, but as a means to show him she was his superior as he had, as yet, to use hers, "I might agree." I couldn't tell if she was delighting privately in this scene or if she simply was an automaton without emotion or empathy. Whatever the case, I knew where this was going and grit my teeth against the pending obvious. "However." Lund shrugged a bare motion of her narrow shoulders, the whisper of velvet from her cloak shivering down to the hem. "The Hayle coven's disregard for the health and wellbeing of our Council and all witches cannot be ignored."

"Surely Ms. Hayle's arrival and decision to join Coven Hall is proof that it is her desire for her coven to change their approach." Professor Carista's brighter tone had an edge to it that she tempered after a quick look from her counterpart. "Seeing as she is heir to her family's magic."

I held in my private wince as the Headmistress's lips curved upward in the nastiest, coldest and most satisfied smile I'd ever seen on anyone's face.

"Ah," she said, dropping another finger. "We get to the heart of the matter. That being Ms. Hayle *isn't* heir to her coven." I didn't respond, doing my best to gather all of my personal commitment and confidence to me and use it like a shield. I'd grown up the daughter of Mahalia Hayle. If the Headmistress thought she could intimidate or bully me, she had no idea what I was accustomed to. I do hope my attempt to maintain my constant expression succeeded even as she carried on to the stricken and surprised expressions on the faces of the two professors. "Are you, Ms. Hayle?"

"I am not," I said, clear and crisp.

"Nor," the Headmistress said, "are you a Hayle witch any longer." Carista gasped as Lund went on, ignoring her reaction. "Are you, Ethpeal Elizabette?"

"I am not," I said in the exact same tone as before.

Both professors seemed to sag, David Gilleland's hand falling on Kate Carista's shoulder.

They knew something I carried as a concern I'd dispelled when the wards allowed me unimpeded entrance, though it was obvious I'd come here to Coven Hall with the correct conception, now confirmed and about to be explained to me by a witch who hated me or my mother or my family—not that it mattered which—in detail.

And with obvious cruel joy.

"Then I must deny your application to Coven Hall," she said, finally coming to stand in front of me, looking up at me with her black eyes full of hate and her lips a thin slashing line as she did her best to seal my fate. "All registrants must be members in good standing of *respected* families." She stressed that purposely, of course. Before delivering what, I was sure, she thought of as her death blow. "But, before I send you away, Ms. Hayle, I must first summon the Enforcers to look into your present circumstance."

Was she going to try to hold Mahalia's actions against me? I was done allowing my mother to ruin my life, thank you.

"On what grounds, Headmistress?" I barely contained GrandMum Burdie's fury, the part of her I carried thrashing violently in response, only Great-Gran Thaddea's power keeping her contained, though even that echo of the witch who was had come to the end of her tether. Only my utter refusal to allow this woman before me an iota of satisfaction held my spine firm and my temper in check.

Lund reached out one finger, her power sparking against my shields, shivering over that which I held inside me.

"You carry Hayle magic with you," she said. "Despite your removal from your family. So, tell me, Ethpeal." She leaned in, eyes narrowing and power now pushing hard against me. "Why shouldn't I call the Enforcers on a witch who's stolen magic from the family who no longer wants her?"

CHAPTER THREE

I had an explanation, naturally, though I was equally positive Lund wouldn't accept my version of events as I was that she would ensure I never, ever attended Coven Hall for as long as she was Headmistress.

Imagine my surprise when Professor Gilleland closed the gap between himself and Lund only to pause at her side, taller than both of us, almost a head over his Headmistress, kindness in his dark eyes as he quickly intervened.

"I doubt Enforcer interference is necessary," he said. "We both know witches removed from their coven retain some influence from that family's magic, especially one born into that family. She could no more shed herself entirely of the touch of the Hayles than she could her own personal power."

Lund didn't divert her attention from me, but the way her lips compressed further, turning downward, told me that the professor had just come between her and some plan she had to destroy me utterly. I almost wished he'd remained silent, as grateful as I was for his intervention, if only to ensure his safety on the matter. Little did Lund know—or perhaps, didn't care—that I had alternatives to her decision I had hoped I could avoid but now understood would be necessary.

Nepotism was my mother's choice of influence, not mine, but perhaps I wasn't as above her tactics as I thought I was.

"You may go." Lund seemed to have decided my fate and waved casually in my direction, turning her back on me, long, black hair shining over the dull velvet of her cloak, the deep purple and gold piping twisting into a tornado of flame up the center from the hem to disappear under her shimmering locks. "May you never darken the doorway of Coven Hall again. Good day, Miss Hayle."

Witch. GrandMum didn't often speak, not in words, but that one made it through, and she meant it in the most derogatory way possible. While I agreed with her assessment, there was nothing I could do at the moment but sort myself out and exit in as stately and composed a way as was available to me.

Thankfully, I wasn't alone, and, despite his Headmistress and her obvious distaste, Professor Gilleland took matters in hand, guiding me with a subtle gesture toward the door he'd entered through. I strode without stumbling to the exit, turning to glance back, realizing the doorway into Coven Hall was gone and only an empty wall remained. He'd saved me from the embarrassment of turning to go and finding the way closed to me, so I had one more thing to be grateful for.

Professor Carista seemed to have no compunction about touching me, grasping my hand and leading me out the door despite my trajectory in that direction. I had just touched foot on the carpeting of the small anteroom on the other side of the door when I heard the way thud shut behind me, turning to find both professors exhaling and shaking their heads before fixing me with unhappy expressions.

"I'm so sorry, my dear," Carista said, her hazel eyes bright with green flecks of power that shimmered through them in her agitation. More emerald sparks fell from her hands as she wrung them, twisting lines lighting her auburn hair. "This is ridiculous."

"But it *is* the law." Gilleland sighed softly, nodding to me, kindness on his face unwavering but regret there, too, as he gently touched my elbow before dropping his arm, parting the front of his robe to tuck his hands into the pockets of his suit trousers. "How unfortunate for you, Ms. Hayle, and no doubt a dreadful tale to be told behind it. I'm sorry we were uninformed and that your journey ended this way."

"You're both too kind," I said.

"Not at all." Gilleland shrugged, chuckling a little. "To be honest, you're wondering why we're here at all, no doubt. Speaking for you?"

I had to admit that question crossed my mind. "Word travels quickly, I take it."

Carista shrugged. "The moment you passed the wards, we knew you were here." She blanched somewhat as though guilty over that truth while I silently kicked myself for my lack of foresight. Of course, Lund knew I was coming, had likely prepared herself for that confrontation I'd just endured.

"It's apparent to me my former family," that truth still choked me somewhat, but the words came out nonetheless steady and strong, "is unwelcome in many circles. I had hoped my freedom from them meant an opportunity here. Had I known being covenless prevents me from attending, I never would have attempted it without making some connection to a family for that purpose."

"I doubt it would have mattered." Carista made a soft sound of frustration, full lips pursed, the green sparks fading somewhat but her irritation far from banished. "It's unfair and you deserve a chance to attend Coven Hall."

"You may not be aware," Gilleland said, "but the Hayle family's trajectory has been somewhat of a source of conversation for many years." A nice way to identify gossip, but I nodded. "When we felt your arrival, I knew immediately you'd have issues with our Headmistress." He glanced back over his shoulder at the closed door. "I wish I'd been informed of your circumstances. My apologies, I did try to locate you before you entered the Hall, but you were elusive." He waved off his own words with a soft sigh. "The point being, there are those of us who would encourage you, especially when we thought you stood as heir, to not just attend Coven Hall but return the Hayle family to the fold."

Everyone had an agenda. "I understand," I said.

"Thank you for your honesty." He could have made up some excuse. It said a lot about him, and his nodding counterpart, that he was willing to be open about his intentions. "I'm sorry to disappoint." He waved that off as I went on. "You weren't concerned my attendance was some kind of attempt by my mother to recruit more witches?" That had been her driving force before she'd taken control of the family, working through and around my grandmother when Lilibeth held the family's power. Thanks to my mother, the Hayles were the strongest coven on the continent. At least, if Mahalia was to be believed and I had no reason to think otherwise. Why else would I be met with such resistance? My pride in my family had always been secondary to my concern about how my mother planned to use the power she'd gathered to her.

"There are those," Gilleland said with great care, "who certainly were."

"Ninnies." Carista tossed her hair, tsking, patting one of my hands with her own. She seemed to have no reservations, at least, and the familiarity of physical contact allowed no dissembling, her authenticity reinforced with every touch. "Because you're obviously here to undermine everything Coven Hall stands for while stripping other families of every able-bodied young witch of your generation." Dear elements, was that what people were thinking? I know I must have blanched, my fury at my mother a burning coal in my gut that the professor didn't seem to notice she'd lit with her words. Instead, she turned to her counterpart. "What are we going to do, David?"

I knew what *I* was going to do. Before he could reply, I raised my chin again and nodded to them both. "Thank you for your kindness," I said, "and your intervention. If you'll excuse me." I know I should have lingered, perhaps, that decorum and gratitude suggested giving them something more emotional in response to their championing. Such extra effort might even have helped me more down the road, but I simply couldn't stand being there a moment longer.

The stairwell echoed with my footsteps as I rushed down them, the three floors to the Yard feeling like they took forever while flying by at the same time. When I emerged out into the light, the now brisk air of the late morning chilled after the storm's passing signaling a change in the seasons as though a switch had been flipped, I instantly gained my bearings, leaving the door of Massachusetts Hall and the Headmistress's office behind me, making a straight line for the other side of the Yard and the big, white building where John Harvard's statue stood. I didn't take the time to run my fingers over his shoe for luck, instead marching directly up the steps to the front door and through. Magic engulfed me as soon as I spun and headed again to the left as I had at the library, passing through the wards that led into the domain of the North American Witches Council.

The building didn't change, tall, echoing stone halls unaltered, but the entire feeling of the place shifted, the power of the Council engulfing me. I knew where I was going, had already sought out directions to her office. Planning ahead had meant contingencies upon possibilities beyond roadblocks and while I knew Sassafras would have teased me for my excessive need for next steps, I was glad I'd done so as I pushed my way without pause through a tall door and into a small office near the end of the hallway.

The elderly witch behind the desk looked up through her round glasses in surprise, leaping to her feet as I attempted to carry on to the next door ahead of me. She moved with surprising speed and nimbleness for someone of her obviously advanced age, eyeing me up with her wrinkles tightening around her lips and gaze, power surging to block my way. Her magic was that of the Council and no matter how much Burdie wanted me to force my way through, I knew I had no other choice than to contend with this next obstacle.

"Ethpeal Hayle," I said before the witch could speak. "Here to see Council Leader Gordon."

She spluttered a moment before gathering herself. "You don't have an appointment."

I almost laughed in her face. Not out of amusement, no, not that. Instead, the sheer frustration of my situation had caught up with me and despite my careful plans and choices laid out before me, that burning ember in my stomach had lit a fire inside me I wasn't expecting. All of my unattended fury at my mother, all of the burden of my almost eighteen years unable to act, unable to take the steps I needed to right the wrongs against my bloodline, culminated in that small, old witch's attempt to keep me from getting what I wanted.

Softly, Thaddea whispered while Burdie's snort of derision underscored that one word.

"I do not," I said, though I admit my tone was crisp and my patience all but worn away. Thank goodness for Great-Gran, I must say, or the sorry biddy would have found herself on the floor in a heap and I, likely, in the custody of an Enforcer. "However, if you would *please*," I said please, though perhaps not like I meant it, sentiment present or not, "tell the Council Leader I have come to speak to her, I know she'll admit me."

The witch before me might have been small and elderly, but she had clearly been in this job for a very long time and wasn't about to be bullied. "You have to have an appointment," she said.

While despair burst the bubble of my anger inside me and almost—almost—left me on my knees.

If it weren't for the door in question opening and the slight, blonde witch on the other side who took one look at me and cried out in surprise. "Ethpeal?"

"Auntie Di," I said while the old witch before me paled to gray. "Sorry to be a bother but I need your help."

CHAPTER FOUR

She ushered me inside immediately with a quiet, "Some tea and sandwiches, Marietta, if you don't mind," before closing the door behind her. I'd already thrown my bag into a leather chair, the crackle of the fire in the large hearth casting warmth in the chill of the room. I was used to tall ceilings and extravagant spaces, but there was a welcoming feeling to Di Gordon's office I wasn't expecting, and it freed me from the rigid control I'd been under, almost too much.

"Ethpeal." I spun on her, tossing my hands, turning then to pace past the fireplace while Auburdeen's old friend watched me do so. "My dear, I heard what happened."

I stopped pacing long enough to meet her eyes. "I'm sorry about the Auntie thing." We'd never actually met, after all, though I'd corresponded with her on a few occasions. "I hadn't intended to impose on you, Leader Gordon."

She came to my side and took my hands in hers, the warmth of her smile and the gentleness of her touch almost my undoing. The Council's power had no reservations about me, engulfing me in its kindness and support while I finally sank into the small divan by the fire, the leader of the North American Witches Council sitting beside me. She was older than she looked, already into her eighties as Burdie would have been if my mother hadn't murdered her. But that was a fury to contemplate another time. Di Gordon had held her position originally for almost two decades, returning to leadership after retiring at the tragic death of her successor. Sassafras had been openly honest that he believed my mother responsible both for Ila Onimara and her Enforcer leader, Shale Courtney's, terrible passing from mysterious illness. Gordon had held the role yet again, in this place another twenty years, the Council's power maintaining her like no other. A celebrated and powerful witch of good heart and intention, she'd never been challenged and, despite my mother's attempts to isolate me from any magic but her own, had always been kind and generous to me.

Any other leader might have acted against Mahalia and the Hayle family. Instead, out of respect for her relationship with my grandmum and, unsurprisingly, Sassafras, Di Gordon had done her best to not only protect my family but me, ultimately.

Which was why I hated so much to burden her with my troubles.

"Let me guess," she said. "Headmistress Lund turned you away from Coven Hall." She sighed and sat back, blue eyes locked on the fire, still holding my hand and forcing me to settle into the cushions as well, tucked against her like she was an old friend of mine, not Burdie's. "I wish you'd told me you were coming, is all. I could have made arrangements."

"My troubles aren't your responsibility." I tsked then. "I've brought them to your door regardless."

She laughed a little, stroking back a lock of my hair. "You feel like her, you know." Tears lit her eyes for a moment. "I miss Burdie very much, Ethpeal." Her sadness vanished as she chuckled deeper. "Not even Auburdeen Hayle would have had the temerity to march into NAWC headquarters and demand to see me. What a witch you will be one day." Di sat up straighter as her assistant entered. The elderly Marietta didn't say a word, though she didn't spare me a moment of notice before setting a tray on the small table beside the fire and exiting, closing the door behind her. If it was odd to you that I found myself served tea and delicious ham sandwiches from the hands of the most powerful witch on the continent, know it was just as odd for me.

"Lund won't let me enroll," I said after devouring a pair of triangles, realizing how hungry I was only after I'd taken a tentative nibble. The complaint in my tone had me stiffening and pulling myself together. "I didn't know I had to be part of a family to do so."

Di nodded, sipping her own tea. "From what I understand, it is a rule, but it's never enforced. She's pulling out the stops, make no mistake. And with good enough reason, I'm afraid." Her cup tinkled against her saucer as she set the pair together in her lap. "Your mother has so much to answer for, Ethpeal. I had hoped you would be the one to ensure she did so."

I didn't respond to that because that made two of us. "I take it she somehow personally injured or insulted the Headmistress."

"Her family, yes." Di set aside her cup and

stared into the fire. "Mahalia recruited a number of members from Kirstin's coven and left them so small and so few that her leader mother had to appeal to a larger family to take them on or risk losing what little magic they retained. She blames Mahalia—and you, naturally—for the loss of her family's status and her mother's subsequent passing after she was forced to give up what remained of their coven's essence to the family that took them on."

No need to wince or feel shame. I had more than enough of that to bear already. It was hardly a new story, one that I'd uncovered time and again and that Sassafras and I had agreed would be a priority when I took over as leader of the Hayle coven. Amends I'd now never have the chance to see come to life.

Di patted my hands again, smiling, though sad. "I have no doubt when you do return to the Hayle coven one day and take over as leader, you will ensure your mother's legacy is not that of brutal and malevolent dominance but put the power she coerced to good use."

I shook my head, staring down into my tea. "I won't be returning," I said. "My sister, Belvah, is now heir and I won't depose her." I would not be my mother. Besides, Sassafras's capable paws cradled my baby sister and his power and knowledge and heart would shape her from here on in. Despite the weakened and sickly baby that she been born, I had to believe he would sustain her and, when the time came, help her when my mother finally died.

Was it wrong I had a moment of hateful wishing that day would come soon?

Di's gasp had me stiffening, though her touch remained kind even as the Council power hugged me gently, its sorrow her sorrow. "My dear," she said. That was all, her grief for me in those two words more than I could take.

I pulled away from her and set my own cup aside, shoving down the tears her kindness roused. I couldn't afford to be weak right now. "That brings me to you," I said. "I need help. I want to be an Enforcer."

Di nodded then, accepting my choice both of my future and my unwillingness to talk about my decision further, standing abruptly and pulling me up next to her. She was tiny, barely five feet to my five-foot-eight, but her vigor belied her age and her smile had me hoping perhaps this was the right choice after all.

"Let me see what I can do for you," she said, sparks of rebellion in her eyes. "I owe Burdie

Hayle, Ethpeal, more than I could ever have repaid her or any of her lineage." I felt grandmum's echo stir inside me in response and was startled when she seized control and embraced the Council Leader.

No more so than when Di hugged me enthusiastically back.

"Well then," she laughed as she let me go, blinking tears. "Let's find you a place to stay on campus until we have this sorted out."

Burdie sighed softly inside me while I simply nodded in return and wondered at her ability to take me over like that. Was it mere weakness on my part? If so, so be it. But if not? I had to be cautious moving forward. The magical gifts Sassafras gave me, that my two ancestors lent me, had come in handy up until now. But this was my life and my path to walk and if I had to give them up in order to walk it…

So be it.

Chapter Five

Council Leader Gordon personally installed me in my temporary quarters, just down the wing from her own, though I had no illusions about how available she'd be to me if her assistant had anything to say about it. Not that I intended to outstay my welcome. Hopefully, with help I was loathe to ask for (and still rankled over, truth be told), this mess would be a memory before classes began in three days.

Hope was not one of my favorite words, but I was willing to at least allow it the opportunity to let me down. I certainly didn't intend to wait around to find out if such frivolity could actually work to my advantage, though. Unwilling to admit I had little to no recourse, I could, at the very least, explore my new environment in an attempt to force my luck to change. Perhaps a firm, fast walk around the campus in the cooling air of the early evening would be enough to recharge my flagging intent.

As I strode out into the Yard with the magic of the Council whispering to me at my exit, I had to quickly and decisively fight off a rounding bout of nerves. Not one to normally take to the anxious, I had to accept my fate was in the hands of others, much as it had been most of my life, and this independent escapade might not work out the way I intended. Normally, I would have an alternate plan to keep me moving forward. I'd been forced into such thinking the majority of my life, if only to stay one or two steps ahead of my mother and her plans to ensure my misery. This was the first time, I had to admit even in the quiet, anxious places in my mind, that I didn't have another option.

When had becoming an Enforcer turned into my be all and end all? I inhaled deeply of the September evening air as I followed, without real thought, the small cluster of students heading for a long, decorative-appearing building at the far side of the Yard. I'd been invited to dinner with the Council Leader, but turned her down when Marietta interrupted, not wanting to stir any more controversy than I had already if I could help it. My fate had always been in the hands of a woman I despised no matter the fact she'd birthed me. It was a sure sign of my unsteady state of mind that the sorrow of not knowing my father woke to rear its whining head. I didn't think about the fact I'd been barely five years old when Herman Birch died of mysterious circumstances others whispered about my whole life, if unable to say anything out loud. I was well aware of my mother's propensity for eliminating those she deemed unwelcome and rebellious, and from what I knew of my father, he wasn't much of a prize past the initial requirement he'd fulfilled in getting her pregnant in the first place. So, such musings and childish sorrow about my lack of a patriarchal figure was hardly in keeping with the woman I planned to become, the witch I knew I was destined to be.

Still hurt, though, when I let it.

I found myself entering Annenberg Hall, the main dining venue for the student body already crowded with young people, their eager energy excited, forward-thinking. It made me feel apart from them, their optimism shining in their faces, powered or not. Perhaps it was just my discomfort at suddenly being exposed to so many people— witches and normals alike—but I had a terrible moment of awkwardness that was so uncharacteristic of me I stopped in my tracks and second-guessed my choice to come here at all.

I caught myself almost immediately, pretending to pause for the second time in a short period, taking in the arching ceiling overhead, the carved wooden beams and shining stained glass now darkened as night fell, setting sun no longer illuminating through them.

My schooled expression either did the job I'd hoped or made me look pained, but either way, that moment of false reflection of my surroundings allowed me the time I needed to gather my emotions and steady myself onward.

Like it or not, I was Ethpeal Hayle and despite my mother's terrible reputation, no one would ever convince me that my family wasn't worthy of respect, admiration and, yes, envy. A little arrogance boosting my confidence, I carried on, hands in the pockets of the jacket I'd donned from my luggage, chin up, fighting continually that urge to turn tail and leave. It wasn't until I approached the food counter, surrounded by strangers, that I accepted this new reality was going to take some getting used to. I'd spent my entire life cloistered in the confines of the Hayle coven and our magic. As brave a face as I put on in the case of my mother, what did I know about holding my own in a situation like this one?

It didn't help I noted a few stares, some whispers behind hands, from witches and normals alike, though mostly from those whose auras carried power. How did they know who I was? If they even did, honestly. Arrogance went too far sometimes. Then again, surely word had spread about my ejection from Coven Hall and perhaps even my appeal to the Council Leader? My cheeks warmed, though I firmly shoved down any embarrassment or shame in the actions I'd taken. I would do my best, and if that wasn't enough, well then, so be it.

I would make a new plan. I just needed something in my grumbling stomach first. Because the moment I stepped up to the counter, a tray shoved in my hands by the witch next to me, I realized Di Gordon's sandwiches weren't doing the job any longer and I was starving.

"Don't take the pasta." The young man next to me, my tray savior, winked brilliant blue eyes at me, a big grin cracking open his boyish if handsome face. He barely met my height, round nose wrinkling as he nodded toward the stainless-steel tray of what looked like spaghetti steaming in wait. "Trust me." He shuddered with some drama before laughing. "You'll regret it."

"Thank you for the advice," I said, knowing I sounded prim but not sure how to stop myself. How had I thought I'd fit in here? I had no experience whatsoever with those outside my coven, not without the Hayle power at my beck and call. I'd always been surrounded by those who knew me, knew my lineage, and had never had to confront a stranger alone before. All of my confidence shattered under the pressure of the constant noise of the gathered students, overwhelming me in a flash while I leaned into Burdie and Thaddea who leaped to my defense.

Not that the young man next to me seemed to notice my attitude. He shrugged, blond curls hanging over the collar of his denim jacket. "It's only fair to warn newbies," he said, those amazing eyes of his sparkling. Someone bumped into him from the side, knocking him into me, and the moment our hands touched when he reached out to steady me, I caught my breath.

A black thread leaped between us, one that immediately waked the dark blossom beneath me, and from the way his eyes widened slightly, I wasn't the only one to feel it. A surge of attraction took me over, both of my ancestresses humming softly in surprise and delight at the contact. I shushed them and shoved them aside, shaking off the goosebumps the touch of his hand had raised, pulling away seeming to succeed in quieting the dark power that now fluttered beneath me.

Funny that neither Burdie nor Thaddea seemed as uncomfortable with the instant of connection as I was.

The young man next to me didn't comment, to his credit, at least on what we'd clearly both experienced, nodding to me as I scooted down the line a moment after realizing we were holding up the progress of other students looking for food. My appetite had vanished momentarily, coming back with a vengeance.

"The roast chicken, on the other hand," my companion winked, "is always delicious. Try the potatoes and the carrots."

I found myself accepting my meal from the surly looking woman in the white apron and paper hat, the clunk of the heavy plate now covered in food thudding onto my tray with some finality. I quickly helped myself to cutlery and a napkin, stopping at the last station with surprise to find a young woman behind a cash register.

"I didn't bring money." More embarrassment. Excellent.

"My treat." My knight in blue denim handed

over some kind of card that the young woman stamped twice before handing it back. "Demetrius Strong, at your service."

"Ethpeal Hayle," I managed to blurt, but that was all I managed as another young man interrupted.

"Dee." The newcomer glanced at me with a nervous expression as though I was about to bite him. Despite his superior height and rather impressive shoulder width, it was clear to me he wasn't comfortable in my presence and was intending to ensure his friend didn't linger with me, either. I do admit to a pang of resentment and disappointment, though I accepted it as how, more than likely, my life was going to be the moment anyone discovered who I was.

Until I made my own mark on the world. And then, we'd see.

That thought steadied me and raised my chin again, though Demetrius didn't seem at all concerned about lingering next to me out of the way of the students filing past the register with their own trays of food.

"Jeffery Bryan-Bradford," the smaller blond said, nodding pleasantly to me, "meet Ethpeal Hayle."

"I know who she is." Jeffery stood to one side of

his friend, not exactly glowering at me, but not entirely friendly, either. I had the distinct impression his protective nature was natural to him, and that Demetrius obviously meant a great deal to him. His dark eyes weren't exactly hostile, just careful, however, so perhaps he wasn't so much judging me as making sure his friend was safe.

That almost made me snort, to be honest. Neither of them had any idea how adrift I felt, how lost and rudderless in a sea of strangeness I thought I wanted and now wasn't sure I could handle under the best of circumstances. I didn't get to reassure Jeffery, however, Demetrius carrying on the conversation as though he didn't sense his friend's reticence. Though, how could he possibly miss it?

"Welcome to Coven Hall," Demetrius said, soft tenor warm and authentic. I could sense nothing untoward, no falsehood, and trust me, I was accustomed to ferreting out disingenuous behavior. His witch magic was a conundrum, though, not nearly as powerful as what I was used to, no comparison to the vibrating aura his friend commanded. But what about that darker energy in him that whispered of depths of power I hadn't experienced before? I knew its source, was surprised to realize I knew all along what the darkness in me represented but had been too caught up in my troubles to accept.

Sorcery. He was a sorcerer. And, it seemed, so was I, for what that was worth.

It almost made me doubt him just out of principle, which was hardly fair. Didn't I just come to understand I carried the same power inside me? My liberation from the family magic must have made it possible for it to rise at last, the wards surrounding Harvard's campus the catalyst for its waking.

Then again, I'd done my best being raised by the most horrible of people, so perhaps I could be forgiven for my doubts and suspicions over a magic I knew little about that wasn't unpleasant, requiring the elemental sources of its use to be consumed for it to work at all. What did that say about me and who I was becoming? Not much, and considering I really had only a scrap of a whisper to go on, leaping to conclusions was the last option I needed to choose.

Maybe he could serve to supply information I was apparently going to need to understand what I now had access to.

"I'm not yet registered," I said, that stiffness in my tone remaining despite myself. Why was I challenging him when he was being so kind and was an obvious source of assistance? Because it wasn't his power that had my back up and my internal walls erected. I felt my whole body tensing against the prospect of rejection, waiting for it to come despite myself.

"I'm sure that will be sorted soon." Demetrius carried on like my life's path and the dream I'd allowed myself was merely a breath away and the problems complicating it a speed bump on the road. If only. I felt myself relax somewhat as he prodded his tall friend. "Right, Jeffery?"

The tall, handsome brunette immediately nodded, a reassuring expression crossing his face though he seemed to catch himself and appeared confused even as he spoke. "I'm sure," he said, trailing off into an awkward silence that only increased, though I think only Jeffery and I felt that discomfort. Demetrius kept smiling at me, gentle and interested, head cocking to one side, while that dark power of his emerged again to make a soft offer of connection.

Panic rose in a bubble of uncertainty within me, my inability to look away from his remarkable blue eyes ruffling my feathers like his touch had only a few moments ago. My own blossom of sorcery seemed eager enough to investigate, though with a languidness that felt far too close to physical attraction for me to accept. What was this odd desire? I will admit now, I'd never dated, nor had any wish to. I'd been far too focused on the family drama, on my mother and my family's fate to even consider complicating my life further with those of the opposite sex. Which, I now had to admit to myself as the truly adorable and imminently intimate Demetrius Strong stood there so close to me I could touch him (and wanted to) with a simple outreach of my fingers, I'd failed myself in not exploring that part of me before now. My utter lack of education in matters of the heart might just be my downfall.

CHAPTER SIX

Before I could do just that—fall and perhaps land on my face or backside in humiliation—a young woman's voice interrupted.

"Ethpeal Hayle, as I live and breathe."

My head snapped around immediately, the tone jerking me out of uncertainty and into old habits, though the smile on the blonde girl's lovely face as I spun toward her didn't warrant alarm. At least, not initially. We'd see. Regardless, she was pretty enough on the outside, though I was well aware that looks were often as deceiving as anything else. Ice blue eyes rimmed in perfect mascara, full, perky lips pinked with gloss and abundant, shining curls curving her blonde locks, the attractive young woman nodded to me with a rather regal air that reminded me far too much of my mother—and myself, yes, be fair—to make me entirely comfortable.

"I am," I responded, not trusting myself to elaborate. "And you?"

If she was insulted that I didn't know her name she didn't show it, though the other young woman next to her, a younger and not quite as beautiful copy, frowned at me like she was offended. "Odette Dumont." A hand rose, offered to me, a spark of power there. I almost didn't accept. After all, we were surrounded by normals, and doing magic in their presence was always forbidden. But no one seemed to deem it odd, so I mirrored her action, my hand up, palm exposed.

Magic jumped to my skin, sizzling a little, my own responding with a softer landing. How odd, for a moment I tasted the tang of copper on the back of my tongue, though it was gone so fast I could only assume it was my imagination or hunger.

"Nice to meet you." I did my best not to scrub my hand on the side of my tray to erase the lingering tingle her share had left behind. It wasn't until that moment I realized Demetrius had left me there with Odette and who had to be her sister—

their power and looks were far too connected for anything otherwise—and had taken his tall friend, Jeffery, with him. Why did that suddenly leave me feeling exposed and abandoned? Demetrius didn't owe me anything.

I needed to sort myself out and quickly. If only I had an outcome to lean into, perhaps that would have bolstered me. Instead, adrift and untethered, I struggled to keep my composure while Odette turned and gestured to the young woman who prodded her as though as an afterthought.

"My sister, Naudia." Odette carried on before her younger sibling could finish raising her own hand and I chose to pretend I didn't see. It was easy enough, since as Naudia's fingers rose, a shadow fell over us.

I looked up and found matching icy blue eyes that were Odette's male counter, though their resemblance ended there. While Jeffery had a good set of shoulders, his lean frame was no comparison to the muscular bulk of the six-foot-plus mountain of handsome who stared down at me with a stern but not unkind expression, sharp cheekbones and jawline etching his face into a statue's perfection. His dark hair had been swept back from his forehead, faint hint of shadow on his jaw and tanned cheeks giving him a rather rough-around-the-edges flair I found made my mouth dry for a moment. But it was his power that had me stopping to pay attention, the low undulation of blue magic that I knew immediately, the fire he carried around with him contained but simmering at the surface.

"You're an Enforcer," I blurted. Oh, Ethpeal, how awkward.

"Second year trainee," he said in a voice so deep it made my bones hum. "Ivan Dumont." His head cocked to one side, gaze turning to the two other Dumonts in our presence while my heart skipped a little. "Cousins," he said.

"Ivan." Odette immediately leaned into him, her tray held out to him, a pout forming on her lips. "Carry my dinner?"

He stiffened but nodded, accepting her offering before meeting my eyes again. "I didn't get your name."

"Ethpeal," I said, doing my best to fight the breathlessness he'd roused. This was ridiculous. I was not turning into a simpering girl over a tall and handsome man. I'd been surrounded by tall and handsome men my whole life. Maybe it was the Enforcer power he carried, or perhaps it was my discombobulation, but whatever the reason, I was in a war with myself and now terrified I'd lose before he walked away.

I would *not* lose.

"Naudia, I'm hungry." I hadn't even noticed the other witch standing with the two Dumont girls, only then noting the skinny and rather unremarkable young man who spoke up in his nasal tenor. She waved one hand over her shoulder at him in obvious irritation.

"Not now, Ralph," she snapped.

His sullen expression settled as his muddy brown eyes landed on me like he blamed me for this delay.

"Ethpeal Hayle." Ivan Dumont's lips parted a bit, a smile twisting his handsome face into an even more appealing shape, perfect white teeth flashing as he bowed as best he could over his cousin's food tray. "An honor. I'd heard you were here. I hope we get a chance to talk."

I almost asked him why, because I was a blithering idiot who really had no idea what she was doing. The only thing that stopped my tongue was the look on Odette's face. She might have been beautiful, but there was enough ugly in her it showed the moment her cousin focused his attention on me. I caught the flash of her fury, of her jealousy, and was grateful for the distraction. She might not have been my mother or anywhere near the level of evil that Mahalia Hayle commanded, but here, at least, was a reaction I understood and could use to steady me in a sea of utter uncertainty.

"Perhaps another time." I nodded to him, to Odette and her sister, then turned and walked away, putting distance between me and the Dumonts. My gaze locked with a wave of almost painful gratitude on an empty seat at a small table at the far end of the long, narrow space and I strode toward it, hoping my strong strides didn't look as desperate as they felt.

It was all I could do not to fall into my seat, to take my time spreading my napkin in my lap, not looking, not turning my head to see if anyone was watching me. With a firm grasp on the poise that I'd practiced my entire life, I ate my dinner despite my warring nerves and hunger stirring my stomach into unhappiness and waited until I was done, lips dabbed on the white square I then set aside, before I allowed myself to unclench.

I stood then, composed and contained, leaving the dining hall at the same steady and unrelenting pace. No one tried to stop me or talk to me, and I had to admit I was equally as disappointed in myself and the loss of opportunity to meet others as I was relieved to escape into the evening air without further conversations I wasn't prepared to engage in.

At least I could be grateful to Odette for giving me the returned edge of my lifelong education, though falling back on old habits wasn't my intent. I'd come to Coven Hall to reinvent myself in a time when my mother decided I was no longer welcome. That had been the plan all along and carried me here to a destiny I now discovered might not lead where I'd expected.

But maybe that was for the best. People like Odette and her sister would more than likely have attempted to befriend me, and I wasn't sure I wanted to play that game anymore. Besides, I wasn't a Hayle any longer. Any power I might have, any presence I might command, was mine and mine alone. Since I now understood I had no idea what that even looked like...

I couldn't bear to return to my room, not yet, and instead headed out to explore the campus. It wasn't a big leg stretch, however, the Yard small enough to be frustrating in my need to explore and burn off some nervous energy. I paused at the edge of the campus and looked out across the busy road to the other side, considering an exodus and exploration into what Boston might have to offer. But, as I considered my options, I felt a little hum of power reach out to me and prod me from the edge of the wards guarding the Yard and instantly recognized it. At least, the feeling of it. Because I'd just encountered something like it in the dining hall.

But while Demetrius's sorcery had a darkly welcoming feel, the magic I sensed passing through the wards at that moment?

There was nothing welcoming about it.

CHAPTER SEVEN

I'd been around corruption my entire life, so I knew what unhappy power felt like. There was no mistaking the threatening pressure of whatever and whoever it was had just crossed the wards and into the Yard. But when I reached out on instinct to sample it, to identify the source, it faded from me, dark mist gone in the breeze of the evening.

I shivered inside my coat, seeking out the magic I'd just encountered, finding nothing. It didn't help the two women whose power I carried argued in their fashion over my next course of action. Thaddea's more conservative and cautious needs clashed with her daughter's commanding demand I do something about what I'd just encountered until

I finally sighed and shut them both down.

"Not tonight," I said.

Burdie grumbled while Thaddea's power engulfed me in the loving energy that I'd grown up with. I briefly considered reporting what I'd encountered, hesitant as I stood there on the edge of the witch world and normal. I could go to Di Gordon, of course. But what was it exactly I had to report? Not much, if anything. In fact, without a trace to follow, what proof did I have I'd even encountered it? For all I knew, sorcery was a regular power here and I'd jumped to a specious conclusion out of ignorance. Wouldn't be the first time, now acutely aware my education had been very much lacking. There was a great deal I'd missed out on in the heart of the Hayle coven. This was my chance to learn without drawing attention to myself. The last thing I needed was to make myself even more conspicuous.

I wasn't accustomed to second guessing myself and didn't enjoy the experience even a little bit. Nor the idea that perhaps I'd misjudged the young man I'd met not so long ago. While my powerful attraction to Ivan Dumont felt more physical, there was a magical component to my connection to the adorable young sorcerer I'd encountered that, given distance and a moment to think, appealed to me far more than the hulking mountain of handsome that was the Enforcer trainee. Not that I'd have the chance to find out if either was a good match. Yes, I fell into glum disillusionment in that moment, torn as I was by my feelings of ineffectuality and boundarylessness.

I finally shrugged off the questions in my mind, scowling into the street and squaring my shoulders. "Enough, Ethpeal," I whispered to myself in Sassafras's tone of voice. Funny how it actually made me feel better, not worse. I shed my concern about the sorcery I'd felt. After all, the wards had done nothing to prevent whoever wielded that magic from crossing into the Yard, wards as old as Harvard and Coven Hall, built by witches stronger and more talented than me. Who was I to question that? Never mind Burdie whispered that sorcery trumped witch magic every time and this was something I needed to worry about.

I had my own worries, thank you. No need to make more.

Namely, this mess I'd found myself in. And as the two young men who'd caught my attention, well. There would be time for those kinds of explorations if I managed to pull off a miracle and attend Coven Hall. Otherwise, the point was moot.

Without any real reason to linger and

determined to shift my mood out of the melancholia I'd been existing in since emerging from Lund's office, a mood that had only burdened me more and more as time passed, I stepped through the wards myself, heading into the depths of Boston in search of some kind of distraction and a renewal of confidence.

I found what I was looking for in a billiard hall not far off the first street I crossed and though I had to use a breath of magic to distract the bartender from kicking me out for being underage—illegal, but some risks were worth it—I spent the next several hours firmly and completely trouncing a trio of handsome young men, divesting them of the contents of their wallets while proving that skill was stronger than magic with every shot.

And that yes, indeed, the presence of an attractive selection of the opposite sex had no influence over me whatsoever, and I'd only been experiencing a moment of weakness when it came to Demetrius and Ivan.

I might have influenced the situation in my sheer determination to prove my self-sufficiency, but not the game. Not ever, satisfaction was far too valuable to me to cheat.

My next stop was a small diner on a busy corner, the scent of coffee and confections luring me inside. I paused at the counter, waiting for the primly dressed woman in a pink dress and apron to show me where to sit, when someone brushed against me. The dark blossom beneath me reacted instantly, though as I turned and met the eyes of the haggardly thin woman who stood beside me, it retreated to return to its quiet humming undercurrent.

"Excuse me," she muttered, one hand on the shoulder of the young man beside her, his huge, dark eyes locked on me, pale face as emaciated as hers. The narrow-chested man who lurked behind them seemed as intent as she was, though when I softly prodded all three, I found nothing but the sensation of latent magic.

"Of course." To my surprise, my grandmum seemed suddenly alert and suspicious, though she wouldn't share why. And then there was no time for more, a wave indicating I should follow the waitress to my table.

The small family disappeared into the depths of the diner and from my mind, until I stood to leave, my newly earned money covering the check. My hand brushed something as I walked past another table, sending a small book spinning away to hit the floor with a thud. I almost missed it, my sorcery surging awake in sudden acute attention that had me blinking. I rushed to retrieve the fallen item, embarrassed by the faux pas and my power's reaction, only to have the thin-faced woman try to beat me to the dash. A tingle traced down my fingers from contact with the cover, though it was gone in a flash and so completely I was certain I imagined it. The woman shouldered me rudely aside, her bony hands grasping the small, leather-bound volume and cupping it to her chest, scowl on her face telling me to back off.

I did, quickly and with a muttered apology, though Burdie's acute focus had me wondering just what she found so interesting. I hurried out into the street, grateful to escape, grandmum falling sullenly silent as I did. I rubbed the tips of my fingers together, trying to summon whatever sensation I thought I'd felt, and decided either I'd imagined it after all—a common spark, perhaps, or a nerve ending triggered—or the small family was of a magical kind I hadn't encountered before, and their business wasn't mine to poke my nose into.

By the time I returned to the edge of the Yard and the wards there, I had forgotten all about the incident and was smiling and feeling much better about myself and my situation. Worse came to worse, I could find a career touring the country playing pool. I almost snorted at the idea, though why not? I stopped just outside the barrier, catching my breath as I realized the truth I'd failed to comprehend.

I could go anywhere. Do anything. Why had I tethered myself to a magical future when, in fact, I was free to be whatever I wanted and could—maybe should?—reinvent myself to my own specifications?

The utter weight of that understanding was like a blow and held me in thrall until a pair of giggling girls brushed past me, their attention jerking me free of my moment of shock, though I found myself grinning as I finally pushed forward and crossed the wards into the Yard again, heart beating fast.

Ethpeal Hayle, yes. But who did I want that to be?

ETHPEAL HAYLE. My name repeated back to me at such volume had me stiffening again, this time in rebellion. That feeling was, at least, familiar, my mother's favorite way to address me, ensuring the whole coven felt it when she did so. I wasn't the only one pondering me, it seemed. Lund's mental voice hit me harder than my realization, staggering me for a moment, though I quickly warded against her and shoved back, shoulders aching from the effort as she continued her shouting command. *REPORT TO ME IMMEDIATELY.*

I almost didn't go. I thought about instead marching right back out into the Boston streets and getting lost in the normal world. The aching longing of that idea was so powerful, I actually wavered before reality kicked in.

On my way, I sent back.

Just a little sullen.

Chapter Eight

I'd barely passed through the door to Lund's office before she pounced, and she wasn't alone. It took me a moment to realize it, however, the Headmistress's domineering power thundering against me while I stopped in my tracks and took on the battering magic she threw my way along with a question.

"Where have you been?"

I wasn't expecting that, nor the presence of Professor Gilleland, Professor Carista or, to my complete shock, the sight of Council Leader Gordon sitting on one of the divans.

"Exploring Boston," I said when no one else spoke. "Why?"

"You were not given permission to exit the wards or depart from the Yard," Lund hissed at me while I scowled back. I wasn't doing myself any favors, I knew that, but she'd caught me off guard and I was already struggling with frustration. It didn't help that I'd been fed that odd sense of freedom just moments before, a lack of self-preservation taking me over and a recklessness seeping into its place.

"I didn't know I needed it," I said. "I am, after all, not under your purview, Headmistress Lund, so I wasn't aware you had the right to tell me where to go."

Someone snorted. I didn't catch who, but from the grins on the two professor's faces, it was one of the pair of them. But neither spoke, Lund's fury crossing her face. I watched her inhale, knew the end of my opportunity to be an Enforcer was about to be crushed under the weight of her rage undelivered as, in a fluid motion, Di Gordon rose and interrupted her before she could even speak.

"Ethpeal," the Council Leader said with a short not, "we've been discussing your eligibility for entry into Coven Hall." Not a word about Lund's ridiculous attempt at control, enough warning in the older woman's steady and confident gaze I accepted her suggestion I keep my mouth shut before I got myself in further trouble adding to the simmering resentment I now bore for the Headmistress.

And no, it wasn't lost on me I was likely transferring my strong dislike for my own mother on the domineering woman who was doing her best to take Mahalia's place as the boss of me.

"As I already told you," Lund snarled at Gordon. Stopped before she could finish while the Council Leader turned to face her. Blanched a little then schooled her expression with great effort, tone shifting to more respectful if still with an edge. "Council Leader Gordon," Lund said, "the rules are clear, as you know. And the law is the law. Students must be members of covens in order to be admitted into Coven Hall."

"Exceptions have been made," Professor Gilleland spoke up immediately. "Several, in fact, in the last two decades." His eyes met mine for a moment and his lips twisted, a selection of scrolls appearing in his hands, two more floating in front of Carista. Here was the snorter, no doubt about it, though his tone remained smooth and reassuring. "It would be a shame for a powerful and talented young witch to be turned away from our institution for being removed from her own family by a leader we all know has a malicious nature."

That was a nice way of putting my mother was a horrible person.

"Such exceptions are at the discretion of the Headmistress," Lund said somewhat primly, not looking his way, ignoring Gordon's sigh in response. "I'm not convinced Miss Hayle has the fortitude or the attitude," she glared at me to press her point, "to be a productive member of our program."

"And yet, how can she prove otherwise without the opportunity to do so?" Kate Carista's heated words started out hotter and cooled as she pulled herself back, but she didn't stop despite Lund's obvious displeasure. "Ethpeal deserves the right to—"

"Attending Coven Hall is not a *right*," Lund snapped. "It is a *privilege*. And not every witch has that privilege."

That was it, then. Case closed, class dismissed. I found myself almost relieved, oddly, adrift without a plan for the first time in my life.

And enjoying the prospect of not knowing what my next step was. I'd broken myself, it seemed.

Gordon wasn't about to give in, however. "What will it take, Kirstin?" Her voice sounded tired, a little sad.

The Headmistress shrugged a sharp motion of

her shoulders, lips drawn down, hugging her robe about her, skinny frame showing through the heavy velvet. "Permission from Mahalia's lips," she said, "and reinstatement to the Hayle coven." Her dark eyes glittered as she stared at me. Because she knew full well there was no way that was going to happen anytime soon. "Ethpeal must be a full coven member to attend."

"I see." Gordon turned toward me, holding out one hand. I joined her, feeling the heat of magic around me as she engulfed me in the power of the Council's collective energy. "How unfortunate. If you'll excuse us." I let Gordon's magic carry me out of the chamber, the two of us reappearing on the walkway outside of Massachusetts Hall.

Where the elderly Council Leader began to swear so clearly and concisely that I found my eyebrows shooting up and a grin pulling at my lips at her colorful and obviously practiced rant.

"I'm sorry, Ethpeal." Gordon finally exhaled a long and furious breath that ended in one more swear before she stiffened. "There are other institutions," she said. "In other territories. I'm already in talks with my counterpart in Europe. If you're willing, they would like to test you for Enforcer training in London."

That was something I hadn't considered and

had me hesitating. Now that I'd decided freedom was an option, did I really want to carry through? The desperate need in Gordon, the way I felt her magic embrace me, how it was so obvious to Burdie that Gordon felt she'd let me down and was determined to help, ended my newfound liberation movement and had me nodding.

"Thank you," I said. "You have no idea how much we—I appreciate you, Council Leader." Burdie hummed her agreement.

"My dear," Gordon said, shaking her head before turning to leave me there, "you have no idea. Get some rest. I'll let you know when you're leaving."

I watched her go in another wash of magic, hugging myself in the darkness under the glowing light of a lamp post. Obviously, the wards here at the Yard did double duty, distracting normals from the power expended around them. How else could witches and those without magic coexist? I breathed the cool air and let myself dream of life in London, in Europe at large, and found myself smiling into the night.

I would explore the possibility, yes. But now I knew I had options and that excited me more than anything in my life ever had before. I found myself strolling, considering talking to Sassafras and letting him know what was happening. Instead of reaching out, I held off. I just wasn't ready to admit any kind of defeat, not until I had answers. And if that meant I would be walking my own lonely path into the normal world?

He would never approve. Which meant I wanted to be neck-deep in it before he found out because that cat had the sort of epic disappointment tactics that could make a corpse rise from the grave in shame for letting him down.

I had just passed the corner of Widener Library, thinking about how surreal this day had been, when the familiar feeling of that dark sorcery brushed against me again. Unprepared, I didn't react in time to keep Burdie from reaching out and tagging the feeling. But not with my witch magic. With my sorcery.

The dark blossom reacted instantly, the air around me suddenly so cold I saw mist rise from my lips in response as that power drew strength from the very environment. I shivered at the ease of its action, without my education to guide it, and wondered what I was becoming without the family magic to contain this power I never knew I had.

No time for that, Burdie whispered to me, barely audible but her intention clear. *Follow it, Ethpeal.*

Certain I was making a terrible mistake, I

nevertheless did as I was told.

You try saying no to the likes of Auburdeen Hayle and let me know how that goes for you.

CHAPTER NINE

I was so focused on Burdie's order that when I headed out to follow the power she'd tagged with sorcery, I failed to ask any questions. That didn't last, however, the shaken feeling she'd stirred pushing a query out into the vaults of my mind.

Sorcery?

We'll talk later. At least, that was the impression of her communication, close enough. It was obvious to me she wasn't prepared to tell me anything just yet, more accustomed in life to giving orders than having the patience to explain herself to others. And while it was only a part of her power and the echo of her that remained, it was very clear to me that diminished capacity had both frustrated what was left of my grandmum and incensed her to carry out her plan without argument.

I was very close to University Hall by then, surprised to find the power led me toward the NAWC headquarters, though before I had a chance to pass John Harvard on my way around the far corner and the source of the magic I'd sensed and now pursued, I stumbled into a pair of young women who seemed less surprised to see me than I was them.

"It's her!" The smaller of the pair, a delicate blonde with a big smile despite her obvious nervousness, held out both hands to me, grasping mine in her own without permission. I felt Burdie's irritation at the interruption and had to corral my great-grandmother's echo before she could lash out at the young witch who dropped her grip with a bit of a start as though only then realizing what she'd done. "I'm so sorry," she spluttered, pinking in the bright light of the lamp overhead, pretty blue beret framing her face like a wool halo, matching swing coat over her tights and Mary Janes making her appear far older than her seventeen or eighteen years.

I felt Burdie tsk as the power we'd been chasing melted away into the night and vanished, her tag dissipating with distance and, perhaps, lack of contact. I struggled to juggle focus between my now very irate great-grandmother and my own need for decorum since it was obvious the young witch who smiled up at me with faintly trembling lips hadn't intended harm. To the contrary. She seemed so eager to meet me I had to hush Burdie far more aggressively than I intended, feeling power swell, and hoped that act didn't intimidate the now hesitant girl who'd found herself in the middle of a conversation that had nothing to do with her.

"You've been looking for me?" I hoped that didn't come out harshly and from the return of my companion's smile, I succeeded in keeping my tone light and unintimidating.

"You're Ethpeal Hayle," she gushed, looking up for the first time at the tall, slender young woman next to her. I nodded to her companion, the beaming and rather crooked grin from the beanpole of a witch just part of the contrast between the two. Where the smaller, petite girl was perfectly dressed in her navy wool, the long, lean one with her giant head of bushy, dirty-blonde curls and masculine bomber jacket more suited to a football player, jeans and sneakers filling out her less-than-impressive ensemble might have been less put together, but was no less kindly in her expression.

"Varity," she blurted, voice deep for a girl, long-fingered hand stuck out with a tiny scrap of power floating in her hand. "Rhodes. Nice to meet you."

I accepted her offer and returned it with a spark of my own. "And you," I murmured as her companion gushed her own name.

"Deloras Mock-Rhodes," she said, pale blue eyes sparkling. "We're cousins." She giggled at that while Varity shrugged her narrow shoulders inside that bulky letterman jacket of hers.

"On her father's side," she winked at me.

That made me laugh a little, lightened my mood considerably, though Burdie's huffing dissatisfaction lingered. "Of course," I said.

"Saw you at dinner," Varity said, no preamble provided. "Heard Lund gave you the boot."

"*Varity.*" Deloras shot her cousin a look to silence her, but it didn't work.

"That's true," I said. "I'm waiting to hear from Council Leader Gordon. There might be a place for me in London."

Both girls' eyes widened. "Cool," Deloras breathed.

"Lucky," Varity said before shrugging again, both hands now tucked deep into her jacket pockets. "Too bad, though." She did appear disappointed. "Could have used you, Hayle."

An odd sentiment, considering my heritage. "You know exactly who I am and where I come from," I said with some self-deprecation, "so, your disappointment is a bit of a surprise."

"Naw, we're not like that," Varity said as Deloras spoke over her.

"We heard you were banished from your family," she said, eyes wide and sad. "We thought..." she looked up at her cousin who nodded. "We thought you could use a friend or two is all. It can't be easy, being cut off from your coven." Her eyes were suddenly rimmed with tears, her aura heavy with grief.

As I felt myself react to her, I realized I'd been shoving aside my own sorrow and only now felt it struggle to surface, to take over. Which, naturally, I would never allow it to do. That had me clearing my throat and taking a step back from both young women.

"Thank you for your concern," I said.

"Doesn't cost us anything," Varity said. Then squinted at me. "Is it true you were looking at Enforcer training?"

It wouldn't hurt to answer honestly, so I nodded.

"Yeah, we'll really miss you, then," she said. "I'm going into first year. Would have been nice to have you along for the ride."

Now I was jealous and smothered it with cool confidence I suddenly didn't feel. "I wish you the best," I said. "Maybe we'll meet someday down the road when we're both Enforcers." You better believe I now planned to follow through if Gordon did. So contrary, Ethpeal.

"We're going to the café for hot chocolate," Deloras said. Stopped. Waited like there was more that I was supposed to guess. Even as her cousin finally laughed and gave her a gentle shove.

"Come on," Varity said, spinning and staring out, Deloras pausing one long moment before going after her, glancing back at me. Before her cousin paused, smirk still in place. "You coming or not, Hayle?"

I should have gone back to my room and waited there, been a good witch. For all I knew, I would be leaving for London at first light, and I had a busy day already. Besides, Burdie was now prodding me with pins and needles to go after the sorcery she'd tagged, so I had no end of options.

"Lead the way," I told the two Rhodes witches, surprising myself when I chose to follow them instead of going solo.

Maybe I had broken myself after all. Or was that fixed?

Chapter Ten

That was how I found myself seated at a small table in a cute café on the edge off the Yard, inside the wards still but with a normal feeling to it that had me longing for the moment of freedom I'd experienced earlier in the evening. There were sufficient normal students present to reinforce that, though the warmth of the Rhodes magic seemed to welcome me with more enthusiasm than I did it.

If the pair of witches had any idea that they were broadcasting their magic over me they didn't show it, Deloras setting aside her pert little beret and sipping her hot chocolate, Varity gulping the first of two coffees she'd purchased while I'd opted for a peppermint tea. I was surprised to find I found comfort in the pair and when Burdie finally simmered down and allowed me to enjoy their company, I discovered I did.

Maybe there was hope for me yet.

"Lund is such a hard ass." Varity eye rolled as she set down her first empty mug and started in on her second, a jaw-aching amount of sugar pouring in before she stirred it with serious aggression. "I can't believe she won't let you join."

I'd just finished telling them the bare bones of my predicament, so I had nothing to say to that. The sight of Ivan Dumont across the café drinking his own coffee with Odette practically hanging from his arm, Naudia and the young man she'd called Ralph both silent as the elder sister chattered on, had me staring despite myself.

Varity noticed. "You don't want to tangle with them," she said, voice soft and slightly graveled, Deloras nodding with her eyes wide as she seemed to purposely turn away from the sight of the Dumonts.

"I don't know their family," I said. Never mind I knew few families. My mother made sure of that and now I realized just how sheltered I'd been. All of my focused confidence had taken a beating now that I understood just how much I'd missed out on growing up. Maybe London *was* the best choice.

"They're French or some such," Varity said.

"Their family immigrated about fifty years ago," Deloras said, slightly breathless, pink lips pursing to sip her cocoa before she went on. "Rumor is that they were asked to leave the European Council, but no one knows why."

"Probably their arrogance," Varity grumbled. "Think they're better than the rest of us."

I caught Ivan staring at me and turned my head on purpose. He might have been lovely to look at, but I wasn't staying after all. Surely there were handsome Enforcer trainees in London? And why did that prospect suddenly have me grinning?

Definitely broken.

"Do either of you know Demetrius Strong?" I hadn't intended to ask that question and blamed Burdie for prodding me. I knew she was stubborn, heard Sassafras tell me enough stories to that end, but this was getting a bit ridiculous. I shrugged my shoulders in an attempt to adjust myself physically to the pressure I felt her exude only to have her push back while Varity responded with a new grin.

"Oh, yeah, Demetrius," she said in obvious jovial good humor. "Good egg, nice guy, second year Enforcer trainee, like Dufus over there." He was, was he? "Him and Jeffery Bryon-Bradford." She blushed a little, staring at her coffee while

Deloras winked at me.

"I hear he broke up with Cassandra last month," the smaller Rhodes said. "Maybe he's over her enough to be looking for someone new?"

Varity choked on her coffee, shaking her head, blushing deep red. "Don't start with me," she said.

I smiled at their back and forth, wondering at it. I'd never had anything like it and now I really was jealous, but in the best way. I had something like this to look forward to, perhaps?

"Demetrius is a sorcerer," Deloras told me then, nodding like that was amazing to her, blinking rapidly and blushing herself. So, her cousin wasn't the only one with a crush? I was glad I was leaving, then. Despite myself, I rather liked these two Rhodes witches and if I had stayed, maybe I would have hurt Deloras if I'd decided Demetrius was worth exploring that part of me that I'd never let out before. For the best.

Her mention of that power had me pondering what I'd just learned, however, and that Burdie's use of that exact magic meant I had access to sorcery myself. I'd never explored any other power than that of the Hayle family, witch magic my magic. Despite knowing Fey power was also my heritage, this new discovery of the dark blossom had me pondering. But it made sense that someone of Burdie's bloodline might also carry the ability to wield sorcery. It was well enough known in the family my grandmum wielded it, that it led her on adventures before she became leader long ago. But me? Sassafras had never mentioned that he thought I might have it, too. Did that mean he didn't know, either? Not hardly. The wretched Persian didn't hesitate to keep secrets if he deemed it necessary, though this seemed even beyond his frustrating choices. Surely if he knew I had sorcery—a power that could cut through witch magic if the stories were true—he would have made sure I was trained in it.

And yes, to fight my mother. What other reason would there be?

Yet another prospect to be excited about, though, I admit it. I was hanging a lot on the chance Gordon might get me into a school in another territory, though. I really needed to pull back, to guard myself. I found I struggled to do so, however. How odd that this bit of exploration of the world outside the coven—and my realization of liberation—interfered with my ability to suppress my hopes and dreams.

Surely that had to be a good thing. Until my heart was broken. Well, if so, then I would find a way to carry on.

"Poor thing." I hadn't realized how distracted I'd become, returning my attention to the conversation just as Deloras sighed over her cup.

"Who's that?" I felt terribly I'd lost the threat of the chat, but she didn't seem to mind and neither did Varity.

"Demetrius," Deloras said, voice dropping to barely a whisper while she looked around as though expecting him to arrive suddenly and overhear. "His family, such a shame." I blinked, lost, while Varity leaned in and gave me the rest of the information I needed to agree or disagree with Deloras' assessment.

"Their being absorbed," the first year Enforcer trainee told me, "by the Dumonts."

Oh. I see. Then yes, I did agree with Deloras. And yet, I had no doubt in my mind Demetrius Strong wouldn't let something like that get in his way.

Varity was obviously thinking along the same lines as me. "Won't matter once he finishes his training," she said. "We're all Enforcers, no family affiliations, once we take on the black and blue. Just puts him at a disadvantage right now, you see." She nodded the barest bob of her curls toward the Dumont table. "He holds his own though."

Was she suggesting that the Dumonts were

somehow making Demetrius' life difficult? That Ivan was? And why did that rouse protective anger inside me?

Because I'd spent my whole life fighting off the biggest bully in the world, that's why. Which was the source of my deep and fresh excitement now rousing inside me.

When the door opened and an attractive brunette witch strode through, Varity stiffened, eyes flashing as she prodded me.

"You know who that is?" What was that spark in her eyes and why did she seem so excited all of a sudden?

I shook my head, taking in the rather unassuming appearing witch with some curiosity. She was lovely in appearance, had a cheerful smile she used to greet a pair of women at the entry. It wasn't until I opened up to her magic that I gasped in surprise even as Varity spoke again.

"That," she said, "is Professor Lisa Noe-Bradford," she said, "head of the Enforcer trainee program."

I was on my feet and approaching the woman before I could stop myself. Because I might not have been in a position to learn from her, but she was going to know my name before I left.

CHAPTER ELEVEN

It was obvious to me that Noe-Bradford was well aware of my identity as I closed the distance between us, since she didn't show even a flicker of concern at my rapid approach. Nor, however, did she appear concerned or even dismissive, instead smiling kindly at me as I finished the last step and stopped in front of her. I was surprised to find she was slightly shorter than me, lovely face turned upward, welcome in her aura the gentle but energetic feel of a natural healer. I hadn't expected to feel that kind of power from someone who ran the Enforcer training program, though there was nothing soft about her as she extended her hand to me, spark of blue fire in the offing.

I could tell from the startled expressions on her companions' faces they hadn't expected such a move and took it as a good sign, instantly returning the favor. When Noe-Bradford's magic met my palm, mine trading places with it to slide beneath her skin, I felt nothing but welcome and empathy.

If only she knew how close that compassion of hers came to bringing me to my knees, she might have regretted it. I managed to contain myself as she nodded to me with a casual air as though finding me here in this way was nothing out of the ordinary.

"Ethpeal," she said like a good friend might, not someone I'd just met who was clearly my superior. Wait, no, she wasn't and wouldn't be, not unless I was allowed entry into the order. I tried to balance that understanding with the gloom it brought as she went on. "I'm sorry things didn't work out for you here. I was hoping for the chance to test you."

Did everyone at Coven Hall know who I was and what my intent had been? I had to remind myself of Professor Gilleland's reveal, that my entry through the wards had alerted those who needed to know about my presence. I wasn't so sure I was comfortable with that level of familiarity. After all, I'd never had anything like it before, not outside my association with Sassafras and he played things far closer to his own furry chest, something I'd learned as a child to do myself. Even my Aunties who I'd lived with the past few years knew little of the real me or the plans I had. It was now obvious, however, that if I did choose to go to London—if that was an option, ultimately—I would have to accept the fact that my life was no longer going to be as private as I'd managed previously.

"That's kind of you to say," I said, feeling suddenly awkward in her company, knowing that others stared, that the volume of talk in the café had dropped as the gathered witches watched and wondered. I was never one to quail under the focus and attention of others, but they had always been family, at least until now. These were unusual circumstances and I'd been through a great deal in the last few days, so I really needed to give myself some credit for remaining upright and coherent, didn't I?

"Not at all," Noe-Bradford said, the faintest frown creasing her brow, though her eyes remained kind. "I'm sure wherever you land, you'll find your feet, Ethpeal." She moved past me and crossed to the food counter, and I let her go, though my feet wanted me to pursue her. I realized as I turned and headed back to the table it wasn't actually me driving me to request her attention. Burdie prodded me sharply enough as I sat, I hissed at the pointed poke, frowning as her meaning surfaced.

Tell her what we felt.

There was no way by the elements or stars I was doing anything of the sort. Especially when the front door opened and two familiar faces appeared, one towering over the other. The sight of Demetrius Strong and Jeffery Bryon-Bradford had me wondering about what I had sensed, after all, and pondering the source of whatever it was Burdie felt.

Even as she shuddered inside me, and the tag flared to life.

Leading right to Demetrius.

I was so shocked by this revelation I barely managed to keep my ancestress from lashing out at the young sorcerer who waved at our little group but carried on with Jeffery at his side. I barely heard another word Varity or Deloras said as Burdie fought me for my attention. I swear to you, if it hadn't been for the equal pressure that was Thaddea inside me, stepping between her daughter's power and my own, I'm certain I would have leaped to my feet and confronted the adorable young sorcerer then and there instead of remaining rigid in my seat, feeling the two powers within struggle over the right to tell me what to do.

That was the real end of the conversation, ultimately.

Enough. I rarely addressed either of them directly. I'd not often had reason to and, honestly, aside from occasional squabbles they entertained over my mother, the family magic had been more than sufficient in containing the two scraps of echoes and the residual magic I'd been granted through Sassafras' gift of power. I'd only become acutely aware of just what price that power demanded since Mahalia cut me off from the coven, Sass's attempt to shore up my own loss of magic only exacerbating the issue. That moment was, however, a deciding one for me.

Don't make me regret accepting you, I sent within.

That silenced both of them, though Thaddea's presence felt more soothing than her daughter's shocked hurt. Burdie retreated, redheaded temper undiminished and, perhaps, even more uncontained without the full embodiment of who she'd been to wrangle it. And as much as I regretted speaking to her that way when she turned her back on me and hunkered down to sulk, I knew if I didn't get control of this situation, I wouldn't be going to Enforcer school on any continent.

I'd be in the loony bin.

I only vaguely recalled the conversation carrying

on next to me, but when I finally did return to it, both Varity and Deloras seemed oblivious to my mental absence. In fact, they both seemed even more agreeable toward me than before and, when I noticed Demetrius and Jeffery exiting, seemed sad to see me go as I rose to pursue them.

"Don't leave without saying goodbye," Varity said, still on her second coffee.

"We want to see you off to your next adventure," Deloras said, standing to hug me.

How unusually lovely. I embraced her back only because I was too distracted by the departing sorcerer to think otherwise and had a moment of melty emotion at the tightness of her squeeze. Physical affection had been so rare in my life that I found myself tearing up over this brief but oddly meaningful connection I'd made with the two young witches.

"I'll be sure to do so," I said. "Thank you for your kindness. I really should go." I headed out at a clip, head down, hands in my pockets, not wanting them to see the shine in my eyes even as I hurried to catch up with Demetrius and his friend. While going after him to ask questions might have been exactly what Burdie ordered, I had no doubt in my mind I was running from the feelings the two girls had roused in me.

I barely knew them, but I was suddenly very sad to leave.

My strides carried me quickly in the path of the Enforcer trainee friends, the tag Burdie tied to Demetrius leading me onward. It wasn't until I reached a branch in the path I realized the boys had parted ways, the taller form of Jeffery departing toward the dorms while Demetrius hurried into the darkness out of the light of the tall lampposts. That had me concerned all over again, though surely, he was allowed a shortcut? Clearly, I was taking Burdie's influence too much to heart and considered doing as I'd told Varity and Deloras and simply retreating to my quarters to sleep and prepare for possible good news from Gordon.

Instead, I stumbled to a halt a moment later as I caught sight of Demetrius slinking out of the dark and approach what looked like a small chapel. I was far too close to hide my approach by then, one foot sending a rock skipping out onto the walkway he'd just entered. Demetrius turned quickly and stilled, though he didn't retreat as I joined him with a rather hangdog expression despite my grandmum's prodding to hurry up and confront him already. Turned out when I was doing what she asked, all was forgiven, and her pouting ended with my pursuit.

"Ethpeal." He didn't seem happy to see me, though he wasn't exactly upset, either.

"Hello again," I said. And paused, unsure how to broach the subject. It was Thaddea who came up with the words, surprisingly enough. "I'm sorry to follow you like this, but I was hoping I could ask you some questions." He didn't comment. "About sorcery. I'm afraid I know so little about it even though it turns out I have access to it myself." That came out rather genuinely, to my relief, and though he didn't seem keen at the moment, he softened a little.

"You wouldn't," he said. "Witches rarely do. But being cut off from your family's power..." he sighed softly. "There will be things you learn about yourself, things you would never have imagined, that will show up for you now." He almost sounded what, envious? No, eager and clearly understood exactly what I was going through. "I'd love to chat," he said then, closing the distance between us, blue eyes catching the light from the post above, "but not now. I'm meeting someone." I could feel the vibration in the thin witch magic he possessed, though he smothered it quickly in a dark bloom of mist that was sorcery. My own woke to the movement, the black blossom waking beneath me, almost as though the petals of some foreign flower unfolded and waited to see what I needed from them.

"I understand," I said. "I won't be here much longer. I might have to go in the morning." That much was true.

He hesitated another moment, visibly torn, then shrugged. "I'm sorry," he said. "Please, this is important. I'll come looking for you tomorrow. If you're still here, I'm happy to talk."

Burdie prodded me again to confront him, but Thaddea stepped in once more, suggesting otherwise and I took her advice over my great-grandmother's hissing command.

"It was nice to meet you," I said, turning and exiting the light, returning to the shadows. Only this time I took more care with my steps and, breathing life into the blossom beneath me, the sorcery that I could now feel and sought out on purpose, I wrapped myself in the dark mist even as I tucked behind a large oak tree and waited.

Whatever he was up to, whoever he was meeting, I'd be here to see it, even if only to satisfy my own curiosity.

CHAPTER TWELVE

I was already second-guessing my decision to stalk Demetrius by the time I reached the safety of the tree, though the fact he lingered with his shoulders hunched and furtive looks cast behind him from time to time cemented my feet to the ground and kept me from walking away in annoyance at Burdie's insistence he was part of something nefarious.

Fortunately, it didn't take long for those he was waiting for to appear, so I didn't have a prolonged bout of trying to talk myself out of this course of action. Instead, my need to know now thoroughly piqued, I watched as several people in robes hurried toward him. He straightened as they did, nodding to the one in the lead, all of them hooded and impossible to identify. Demetrius didn't hesitate, hands waving in front of him, triggering a wave of blue flame that opened what looked to me like a portal or doorway. The three newcomers followed him through the gap he'd created—was that a stone wall on the other side?—before the fire flickered and went out.

Leaving me to stare at the now empty and unassuming spot in front of the small chapel with no more answers than I'd had, only more questions.

It was frankly hard not to be concerned that the young sorcerer was involved in something he shouldn't be, though without proof I was simply speculating about someone I barely knew. My gut instinct, however, had me anxious. Or perhaps it was more so Burdie's insistence I investigate further that was the real source of my trouble. I stayed where I was for at least a half hour, waiting for Demetrius and his companions to return, but to no avail. Finally, feeling a mix of foolish for my unfounded suspicions and lurking while my stomach churned with nervous energy that I was allowing something terrible to unfold and had done nothing to stop it, I spun and marched toward University Hall.

My attempt to speak to Leader Gordon was cut

off the moment I approached her door just down the hall from mine. The way to her quarters was warded, a simple message informing anyone who approached she was unavailable stopping me in my tracks while grandmum growled her frustration in my mind.

There was nothing to be done, however, and like it or not, I really had no reason to question Demetrius' motives aside from a suspicion based on magic I carried from a woman who died before I was born.

That didn't stop Burdie from prodding me to exit the hall one more time and quite frankly I wasn't ready to sleep just yet, despite the seemingly endless day I'd just had. Instead, I hurried across the Yard to Massachusetts Hall and the only other person I could think of who might have insight.

I barely touched foot on the step when Headmistress Lund's power rejected me. She must have warded the building against me specifically because I rebounded from the power planted in my way like I'd just walked face-first into a giant balloon. It didn't hurt, not physically, but you can imagine I was swearing just a little—just a little, mind you—from the utter arrogance of the witch's childish choice.

Fine. If Demetrius Strong was up to something

that had negative repercussions for Coven Hall, so be it. Let Lund deal with it for all I cared. She had made this particular bed of hers with resentment and bitterness and she could lie in it and smother.

I turned away, jaw aching from clenching it, the familiar burbling of bile and fury inside me a reminder that it wasn't just Mahalia Hayle who could make me feel small and unwanted. I was so wrapped up in that well-known spiral, I failed to realize I wasn't alone until I almost ran into Kate Carista.

"Ethpeal." She'd clearly seen me, concern on her face, in her eyes, as she grasped for my upper arms with both hands to stop our collision. I almost jerked away from her, though none of this was her fault and surely, she deserved better. She let me go before I could react badly, however, nodding to me with such compassion I sagged at the sight.

"Sorry," I said.

"You have nothing to be sorry for." Professor Carista shook her head with a frown creasing a line between her brows, lips twisted as she glared at the front steps to the hall. "Her, on the other hand." She tossed her head then sighed, offering her hand this time instead of touching me without permission. "You've been through so much, Ethpeal." How did she know? "When we heard you were banished from your family, we'd hoped you might end up here."

I had no idea. But my current circumstance wasn't the problem. "I saw something," I blurted to her. Stopped and pursed my lips against saying any more. Then went on regardless, because what was the worst they could do, kick me out? And she seemed amenable to what I had to say, immediately perking at my statement. "It has me worried."

"Can you be more specific?" No judgment, not a scrap, only curiosity and caring. That gave me the encouragement I needed to go on.

"Sorcery," I said. "I think someone is using sorcery to bypass the wards." There was more to it, I was sure of it, but I had nothing else. And I was loathe, despite myself, to speak Demetrius' name just in case I was overreacting. For all I knew, his visitors tonight were legitimate, and I was making mountains of molehills thanks to my history and the fact my own mother couldn't be trusted.

Any worry I had the professor wouldn't listen was cast aside as Carista wiggled her still outstretched fingers. Her expression told me she believed me, a rather baffling thing to me, understandable or not. "Come," she said, command in her tone, a small flower sparkling with magic from the cuff of her sleeve, revealing what had to be a tattoo, petals shining with power before the sparks faded, leaving the pattern behind. "We need to talk to David."

I went with her, though I didn't take her offered hand, striding along beside her to the other end of the Yard. A moment later I was up the steps and into a building I didn't know, Carista's magic making our presence obvious, though the tall, angular-featured man with bright green eyes and feeling of Fey magic surprised me.

"Marcus," Carista said, nodding to the beautiful stranger as his gaze passed from her to me and back again. "We're here for David."

His hesitation wasn't lost on me, especially when he frowned when his emerald eyes settled on my face. "It's late, Kate."

She wasn't taking no for an answer, pushing her way through the door and inside, past him. He was forced to step away, watching and not protesting while Carista carried on with me trailing behind her. She did pause in the entry of what appeared to be an apartment, single light overhead barely pushing back the shadows of the rest of the house, spinning on the man she named Marcus with her hands on her hips.

"It's important," she said.

He didn't get to protest, the sound of footfalls

coming from an open doorway on our right quickly revealing the tall figure of Professor David Gilleland. He raised one hand to me, to Carista, while Marcus closed the door behind us.

"Welcome." The professor smiled at me, though when he turned to his fellow teacher, his head tilted, dark curls catching the light. "I take it this isn't a social call."

"We need a moment," she said, then stopped. While Marcus let out a long-suffering sigh.

"I'm going to bed." He marched past us and up the narrow wooden staircase, not looking back, the sound of a door slamming shut at the top echoing back down to us.

"You must forgive my husband." Professor Gilleland gestured for Kate to join him in the room past the door in which he stood, nodding for me to do so as well. "Marcus is rather protective of me and our time together."

"I'm sorry about the intrusion, professor," I said.

"Not at all, Ethpeal." He followed me into the room, what turned out to be a library/study combination, with tall, built-in bookcases crammed with volumes, a small desk under the front window covered in papers and a love seat and armchair filling the rest of the space at the far end. I took a seat after he quickly cleared away a stack of books from the sofa's cushions, Carista making her own space as if well accustomed to having to do so.

Gilleland settled into his armchair with a grim smile, steepling his hands in front of him with one knee crossed. He'd shed his heavy velvet robe, the cream button up he wore rolled to his forearms, tie gone along with his jacket, sock feet making me almost grin from the funny pattern of dancing gnomes crisscrossing the toes.

"Can I offer either of you anything?" I shook my head at him, Carista doing the same, his fellow teacher turning to me and touching my hand just a moment before dropping hers to her lap and speaking.

"Ethpeal," she said, "tell David what you told me."

For a moment I considered brushing all of what I'd encountered off and apologizing, heading for my quarters and the hope I'd be leaving in the morning anyway. Surely this was all a misunderstanding, and I was looking for trouble where none existed. I'd come from a particular set of circumstances, after all, that made me prone to paranoia. But even as that thought crossed my mind, I looked first into Carista's eyes and then those of the quietly patient Professor Gilleland and made a choice.

I told them both everything, from my initial encounter upon my arrival that very morning to the second brush with sorcery and the third. I shared my great-grandmother's concern about the feeling of the sorcery, the taint in it, and that she feared it could overpower any wards set without alerting witch magic to its presence. Finally, I told them of the three strangers I witnessed, though at the last moment, and with no small measure of guilt over the choice, I omitted Demetrius' name from the story, instead claiming to be unable to identify who it was that raised the blue flames.

"The Stronghold." Professor Gilleland's kind expression had darkened as I unfolded my tale, leg uncrossing his knee, hands falling to his lap while Carista nodded. "Ethpeal, you said your sorcery recognized the feeling of that power." I nodded. "How long have you had access to that kind of magic?"

I shook my head. "I didn't know I did," I admitted then, positive it would turn them both against me or at least weaken my position to the point they'd brush me off. As they possibly should. Only my tenacity and Burdie's insistence kept me talking. "But it's my guess that once my personal magic was cut off from the family that my other abilities began to surface." I paused another moment, then confessed, "I'm also part Fey."

"Remarkable," Gilleland said without a trace of doubt or accusation.

"We need to talk to Lisa," Carista said. "If one of her students is allowing strangers through the portal into the Stronghold without permission…"

"We don't know for certain what's going on just yet," Gilleland said while Carista huffed at him.

"Undeclared sorcery in use on the grounds is not permitted and you know it." She seemed far more anxious than he was, though Gilleland was clearly taking this seriously.

"I am aware," he said, leaning forward as though that motion could reassure me further. "Though the only reason I hesitate—and in no way am I doubting you, Ethpeal," he said, "is the Stronghold itself."

"What is the Stronghold?" I felt lost, and that feeling rankled.

"Ah, yes, of course." Gilleland sat back again. "The Stronghold is a bit of an anomaly. Another plane, existing alongside ours. It's accessible through Enforcer magic and is used as their base of operations. Coven Hall encompasses all students, but Enforcer trainees reside there will the full members of the order after they are inducted."

"Which means it's warded," I said. "But witch

magic—"

We'd been over that already. "No one truly understands what the Stronghold is," Gilleland said.

"It has its own protections that have nothing to do with the Enforcers," Carista told me, faintest hint of awe in her voice.

"If, as you say, the visitors you encountered earlier weren't welcome in the Stronghold," Gilleland said, "I have no doubt it would have ensured they never gained entry."

"So, I wasted your time after all." I sat back myself, shoulders aching from the tension I'd been holding, regret and embarrassment warming my cheeks and making me wish I'd just gone back to my room. Burdie grumbled but didn't argue with me despite her earlier insistence.

"Not at all," Carista said, glaring at her counterpart. "It's always better safe than sorry. David, we need to tell Lisa regardless."

He nodded abruptly and stood. "Of course," he said. "Ethpeal, thank you for your vigilance." He led us to the door, opening the way outside to me. "Do you need an escort to University Hall?"

I shook my head as Carista lingered with him. "Thanks for listening, professors." I left with my head bowed, hands tucking into the pockets of my jacket, now furious with myself for being such a ninny and with Burdie for putting me in that kind of position.

I heard the door close behind me as I marched with determination for University Hall and my room and sleep. Because I was done with this place, done with the end of the dream I'd had that clearly led me to a foolish leap into suspicion that could have gotten another student in trouble, not just made me look like an idiot. At least I'd kept Demetrius' name out of it.

I had that small miracle to cling to.

Wouldn't you know, my path back to my room led me right past the chapel again? I kept my head turned firmly forward and refused to even contemplate the whispered suggestion Burdie offered up.

"No," I muttered out loud, "GrandMum, I am not going to try to break in and see if sorcery can get past the Stronghold's wards. Please, just stop."

"You in the habit of talking to yourself?" I almost jumped out of my skin as the tall and smirking Varity Rhodes emerged from behind the very tree where I'd spent my own lurking moments. "Or do you just like spying on people?"

"I have no idea what you mean," I said, flushing all over again.

"I saw you here earlier, and you were obviously looking for something that had you worried," Varity said. "Tell me what's going on."

CHAPTER THIRTEEN

It was clear she wasn't going to let me walk away without filling her in, though I really did need to step off. Not that doing the right thing and the thing that compulsion forced me into wasn't too far off my usual, which was why I found myself leaning against the very tree I'd done that lurking behind and told Varity Rhodes everything I'd told the two professors, and more.

Despite the guilt, I shared the identity of Demetrius Strong.

She proved my faith in her immediately, only nodding instead of running off to tell anyone, and when I finished my now efficient telling of my tale, polished after my interaction with the two professors, Varity looked off into the evening distance instead of overreacting as I feared she might.

"There you are." If she planned to say anything, it was cut off by the arrival of Deloras Mock-Rhodes and another witch I didn't know, though her physical and power resemblance to the first year Enforcer trainee I'd just confessed to was close enough of a match they had to be coven mates if not sisters. It had been Deloras who spoke, a bit flustered though smiling still, looking back and forth between me and Varity in obvious curiosity. As for her companion, the other Rhodes witch raised an eyebrow in my direction before addressing Varity.

"Sister," she said, confirming my supposition, "what are you doing out so late? You should be in your dorm room by now." Older sibling, then, and knew who I was, you'd better be sure of it. It was clear from the rippling of her aura she was unhappy to find Varity with me, so despite the two young witches I'd begun to think of in the barest terms as possible friends thanks to their welcome, this Rhodes didn't agree with their choice of companions.

"Violet," Varity said, flashing her sister a smile. "Have you met Ethpeal?"

"I have *not*." Violet tucked her cardigan sweater around her, chin rising, gaze not even flickering in my direction as she addressed her younger sibling with some chill in her voice. While Varity had a masculine, though attractive, appearance to her tall and gangly body, long face and short curls adding to that androgenous feeling, Violet had taken some effort to apply makeup, her shorter stature and thinner body no less boyish in reality but augmented with Violet's attempt to appear feminine. Her long, thin nose gave her a delicately bird-like appearance, while Varity's resembled much more a hunting hawk. That didn't mean Violet was soft, however, if the pressure of her personal wards was any indication, not to mention her obvious disdain that bordered on animosity. I tried not to take it personally as she sniffed and tilted her head. "Back to your dorm, Varity. Now."

To her credit, the younger sister frowned and snorted, so casual in her rebellion I had the impression Violet rarely won these types of arguments. I instantly adored the younger Rhodes for her denial despite myself and had to fight a grin since I felt such kinship with her in that moment I almost laughed.

"Don't be a ninny," Varity said. "Ethpeal, tell the girls what you just told me." She shifted from disdainful amusement at her sister's command to concern and focus all over again.

This time, I had the story down pat and, though I now wished I hadn't, I reluctantly brought Demetrius' name into the matter. It was obvious from Deloras' reaction she was horrified at the thought, eyes widening, both hands covering her mouth as I named him, though Violet only tsked in annoyance.

"As if we can trust a Hayle in any matter of importance. Or otherwise." That was about as rude as things got, I suppose, though she wasn't nearly on par with Headmistress Lund just yet, if close enough. And, frankly, I'd had enough of that kind of attitude at this point, which led me to speaking up when I really should have kept my mouth shut.

"You know nothing of me or my family," I snapped, "and it would serve you well to keep your biases and judgments to yourself, Violet Rhodes."

She blinked at me in such surprise that I felt the moment freeze in place, regret turning to internal dialogue of the self-recriminating kind only tempered by the snorting laugh that erupted from Varity.

"Zip it, sis," my new friend—yes, she was, absolutely, no matter what became of either of us—"and actually *listen* for once."

Violet spluttered, obviously still in the throes of her surprise, while Deloras finally nodded slowly, face crumpled in guilt and concern.

"He's been acting so oddly since he arrived back," she said, voice very low and shaking just a little. "He's usually so patient. But twice now over the last day or so he's been rather short with me." She shook her head, lips trembling. "Not that he has to be nice or anything like that. It's not like he thinks about me that way." I felt my heart break for her as she went on, face paling in the bit of light she landed in as she turned her head. "He apologized both times but hurried off like he had something he was supposed to be doing and I was in the way."

"Regardless," Violet had finally pulled herself together sufficiently to respond, though her cold and superior tone didn't hold the weight it had previously, "you've informed two of our professors and both are on the matter. I tend to agree with Gilleland. The Stronghold would never allow detrimental magic past its wards. You're creating drama over nothing." She barely suppressed a sneer. "Since you're not remaining, Miss Hayle, perhaps you'd be better served minding your own business."

The frustrating part, of course, remained that she wasn't wrong. Still hurt, though.

I didn't get to comment, Violet finally putting her body where her orders were, stepping up and prodding her sister with magic.

"We're done here," she said, addressing Varity directly, cutting me out with an efficient wave of magic that obliterated my ability to even sense the younger Rhodes or Deloras, for that matter. Violet clearly saw me as some kind of threat and was prepared, it seemed, to protect the younger witches from my nefarious intentions. That hurt me all over again, enough I didn't fight her when the pressure built to the point I decided to step back and leave well enough alone.

I'd done my best. It obviously wasn't enough. The story of my life.

Really, Ethpeal, how morose.

Varity resisted despite her sister's attempt to dominate her, though she did sigh and shrug. But instead of walking off immediately as Deloras did, Violet at her side, the younger Rhodes lingered one last moment.

"I'll keep an eye on Demetrius," she said.

"Why?" I didn't mean to blurt that question, or to come across so callous, but her sister had triggered my own worries about myself and my future along with the obvious animosity I knew my mother created in others. Not fair, not by a long shot, but mine to bear out here in the world beyond the coven I'd once belonged to. "Why do you even care what I think?"

Varity blinked then grinned all over again. "It's not your fault your mother is an awful prig," she said. "I knew you were different the moment we met." She did? I would not cry, not weep like a child who never had a real friend outside a furry demon cat who had his own agenda. "Besides, she wouldn't have booted you if you toed the family line, right?" I shook my head. "So, the fact you're a free agent is all the proof I need." She reached out and squeezed my shoulder. "Stay in touch, okay?"

I nodded to her and watched her walk away, her head down, hands in her pockets, lumbering across the Yard in long strides that had her catching up with the other two retreating witches very quickly. There was enough light I saw Violet turn to her sister, the intensity of their conversation as they disappeared into the dark and sighed out the emotion that the whole encounter created.

It was almost midnight by the time I climbed into my temporary bed, and thanks to my endlessly spinning mind, hindered by occasional grumbling from Burdie and interruptions from Thaddea, I barely managed a few hours of sleep. Made worse by dreams, disturbing and yet enticing, in which a woman's face I didn't know but felt I should hovered in my mind. She wasn't either of the echoes I carried, I was certain of that, her black eyes devouring me, endless laughter sending me into a spiral down into darkness only to jerk myself awake time and again.

One thing was certain. Whoever she was, she had some tie to the blossom of power I'd only begun to accept, though when I attempted to tap into it and gain answers, it retreated from me, returning to its rest even if I was unable.

It wasn't long before I finally sat up, blinking into the darkness after a very restless bout of tossing and turning. The moment I cleared my head, I realized the connection I'd been missing in the depths of dream.

I did know her face. I'd seen it once before. It had flashed in my mind, my sorcery awakened by her presence, when I'd encountered that family in the city earlier the evening before. It had happened so fast during the sizzling instant I'd failed to register it until now. What tie had I created to the strangeness that had been that incident? I softly prodded my grandmum, wanting to at least try to converse about this new power I found myself in possession of. Only to find Burdie buried and in full retreat. Whatever her reason for not wanting to interact, I finally stopped trying. With no answers forthcoming and my sorcery offering nothing in way of response, I firmly set aside the question and chalked it up to overwhelm.

Not every magical encounter had something to do with me.

I groaned my way out of bed and prepared myself for my exodus from Coven Hall, sitting on the sofa under the window with my trunk, now back in my possession, packed and ready and my heart heavy and yet hopeful at the same time. With the sun not even yet risen, I couldn't bear lingering there for long and yet again found myself pacing outside into the very early morning.

The first birds had begun their chirping, sky turning just the slightest shade of pale as I crisscrossed the Yard in an attempt to shake off my stress and at least wear out my body further if not my mind.

Wouldn't you know that despite the fact I was done with this place, it wasn't yet done with me? The large oak I'd lingered behind just a few hours before looked somewhat different in the growing dawn but was still easily recognizable.

As was the flare of blue flame that appeared in the exact spot where Demetrius had disappeared the night before. I moved quickly, tucking in behind the trunk, hands pressing to the rough bark as that same sorcerer emerged from the portal, the three hooded figures at his back.

When they fled, the young man I suspected of wrongdoing leading the way, I followed.

In for a penny.

Chapter Fourteen

I stopped before I reached the wards, with no intention of bringing down the wrath of Lund once again despite the fact I was hopefully leaving sometime in the next few hours. Instead, I kept my distance while the three robed figures paused just outside the magical barrier, speaking to Demetrius a moment before they all disappeared in a mist of black power that rapidly dissipated.

Anger woke in me, fury, more to the point, and though it likely shouldn't have been focused on the now rapidly returning young sorcerer, I couldn't control or contain it. After all, it wasn't his fault I'd stumbled on his little misadventure or that my mother was a monster who'd banished me from my family, or even that Lund was denying me the only other future I could even contemplate. And yet, here he was, the only focus I had to vent my frustration and hurt upon.

Lucky him.

He was moving quickly when I stepped out in front of him, my sorcery still blocking me from detection, and only then did I let it fall away, surprised in that moment at its reluctance to retreat. Whatever the case, I kept my attention on the startled young sorcerer who stopped abruptly before slowly approaching me with a frown and a brief glance to either side before he paused before me.

"What are you doing here, Ethpeal?" His voice was low and vibrated with something I couldn't identify, though it didn't feel or sound like anger. Wait, was that anxiety?

"I could ask you the same question." I crossed my arms over my chest, shaking myself now, fully falling into my rage. Call me overtired or overwhelmed, but so be it. "What have you been up to? And who were those people?" I jabbed a finger behind him, without looking away. "And why did you let them into the Stronghold?" I knew I was irrational, had lost control of myself. Such an event would never happen at home. I couldn't have afforded it. Was it my lack of sleep or my loss of connection to the family magic and my future that had me so shaken and disjointed? It didn't matter. The truth was, this was my state of being at the moment and for better or worse, I was showing my weakness to him.

Instead of losing his temper, Demetrius shook his head, his expression a little sad. "This is none of your business."

"I'm tired of hearing that," I snapped. "And of being dismissed. Told I'm unworthy, unwelcome, in the way." Yes, all right, clearly this had little to do with his excursion with strangers and everything to do with my pending exit from Coven Hall. "I know trouble when I'm around it," I said. There, that was better. "And you're neck deep in it, Demetrius. What's going on?"

Like I had the right to demand an answer from him. Again, his reaction was not what I expected, empathy mixing with what I finally realized was admiration crossing his adorable face, lighting his blue eyes. Or was that the finally risen sun? For a long moment, I absorbed that look, took in his visible attraction, the way he smiled at me, with a bit of sadness or not, lost in the instant of connection I felt all over again.

Perhaps more would have come from that

interaction if we hadn't been interrupted. The heavy footfalls of someone running toward us only registered when Jeffery, panting and red-faced, came to a halt next to Demetrius, placing himself at an angle between his friend and me as though I offered some kind of threat.

"Dee." He didn't look down at Demetrius, instead locking eyes with me, not exactly a warning on his face but close enough. "There you are." Jeffery's attempt to be casual wasn't lost on me, nor on his friend, who smiled kindly up at the taller young man without comment. At least, not to him.

"Thank you for your concern, Ethpeal," Demetrius said, "but you're jumping to conclusions that really have nothing to do with you. If you'll excuse us."

Jeffery nodded to me with some surprise, following the sorcerer past me. Or, tried to. I wasn't about to let them both march off, not in this particular mood I found myself in. While my interaction might have softened my anger somewhat, the connection I now felt reinforced and growing, oddly, between our two powers, I was now far more concerned than I should have been in place of my previous fury.

So much so, when he stopped at my physical intrusion, I reached out and grasped his hand, feeling the spiraling blossom of his own sorcery slide across mine with enough force to make me gasp.

"If you're in some kind of trouble," I said, forcing out the words and the focus.

He didn't pull away immediately, letting his power explore mine for a moment. When he finally freed himself, it was with a gentle touch. My hand fell from his, skin parting but the palm of my hand and fingers still tingling as though we remained in full contact.

"It's kind of you to worry," he said, voice very low and soft, leaning toward me, lips by my ear as he spoke. "You have no idea how much that means to me." I shivered as his breath tickled my neck. "But you have your own worries, Ethpeal, and I won't add to them." He leaned away then, nodding to me, smiling sweetly, blue eyes full of sunlight, so much so they seemed almost translucent and bottomless, halo of illumination making his blond curls glow around him like a cherub. "Please, leave it alone. And be well."

I didn't know what to say to that, a bit breathless from this whole ordeal and my sorcery reluctant to retreat, a sense of longing for the touch of his surprising and unnerving enough I backed off. I watched Demetrius and Jeffery walk away, the taller of the two speaking loudly enough I caught his hissing, "Where have you been?" before they were out of earshot.

"You're wasting your time on that one." I spun in surprise to find Ivan Dumont standing behind me, glowering after the disappearing pair of friends. When his blue eyes settled on me, he seemed concerned, closing the distance slowly, as though waiting for me to retreat. "Demetrius Strong isn't worthy of you."

What an odd thing to say. "I'm not sure that's your business, Mr. Dumont."

He shrugged, taking no visible offense, though his expression softened somewhat. While my sorcery had longing for Demetrius, my body seemed to have other ideas.

My goodness, Ivan was a spectacularly handsome young man.

Not to be carried away by physical attraction, but when he drew close enough, I caught the scent of him, I found myself blushing somewhat, softening despite myself. I'd never had this kind of reaction to anyone before, the attractive men in my coven too close to family thanks to the magic that bound us for me to be even remotely interested even if there was no blood relation to speak of. Ivan Dumont was a completely different story, however, not just physically delicious to look at—and he was—but his entire being seemed to radiate some sort of charismatic appeal I caught myself admiring a bit too much.

"You're right about that," Ivan said, deep voice a bit graveled as it lowered in volume and depth, blocking out the morning sun as he stood over me by a head. "Doesn't keep me from worrying about you, though."

"That's kind of you." I fumbled for something else to say, amazed at my lack of poise suddenly and blamed it on my weariness and the stress of the last twenty-four hours and more instead of the odd sensation his attention awoke inside me.

"Not at all." He held out his arm in a rather old-fashioned gesture that had me blushing all over again. "Please, let me escort you back to University Hall."

"That's not necessary," I said.

"I know," he replied, smiling in a way that ended in a crooked and utterly ravishing expression that had me reaching for him despite myself. "But you're about to leave my life forever and I'd like to savor the last few moments by having you all to myself at last."

How very charming and unnerving all at the same time.

We strolled and he chatted while I listened and managed responses that didn't quite make me cringe when I thought about them later, the shift from stressful focus to this unexpected unwinding leaving me disoriented. So much so that by the time Ivan left me on the steps to University Hall, I lingered longer than I planned and even stood and watched him go, admiring his tall, broad-shouldered form going as much as coming.

Not that I'd forgotten my dilemma or the curious worry that was Demetrius Strong, but I have to admit I was grateful for the interlude, even though such an interruption normally would have made me frustrated and annoyed. I caught myself smiling as I entered the wards and almost floated down the hall toward Gordon's office, hoping this feeling boded well.

If only. Instead, as I was ushered into the Council Leader's office by her previously judgmental assistant, I was instantly tense thanks to Marietta's sudden show of empathy toward me. That growing suspicion only increased as I joined Di Gordon at her desk where she watched me enter with an apology written all over her face.

"Bad news, I take it." I fought off the urge to lash out just barely, that hope I'd allowed a place inside me shriveling and dying in a spark of renewed anger that I smothered before it could emerge. I would not cry. I would not rage. I would find another path.

I *would*.

"I'm afraid so," Gordon said, circling her desk to join me, raising one hand to touch me. I took a step back immediately, rigid against her and her sympathy, if only to keep from cracking down the middle. She dropped her attempt to reach out, sorrow and her own frustration now clear on her face and in her magic as it hummed in irritation, the Council's power vibrating under my feet so loudly it made my teeth ache. "While Portia Ologarve and her Council are amenable, the Headmistress of Oxford Hall has considered your admission and opted to deny you registration."

Lund. It had to be. "I take it that goes for other schools as well." There were, after all, many world territories. Surely the Headmistress didn't have the ear or support of all of them?

"I'm still working on it," Gordon said with enough fluster in her voice I almost felt sorry for her. Almost asked her to stop. Should have, perhaps. After all, hadn't I realized I was free to do what I wanted if the answer was no? For whatever reason, I struggled with the truth now, despite my previous awakening. "We'll find you a place,

Ethpeal."

I nodded to her in a tight bob of my head. "Thank you for your time and effort, Leader Gordon."

She sighed deeply, marching forward suddenly to embrace me and I hugged her back. It was a mighty battle I fought then not to burst into tears on her little shoulder and took all I had not to lean into her, to fall to my knees and hug her like a child.

"It will be all right," she whispered to me. "I promised Burdie I would always do my best for her children. Mahalia never allowed that and poor Winnifreth…" I swallowed the tears choking me, throat so tight I couldn't speak. My Auntie Winnifreth had lost her beloved husband and her infant daughter thanks to my mother's actions, and I would never forgive Mahalia for that. It sounded like Di Gordon felt the same. "I will not fail you, child."

I pushed her gently away. "You've done more for me than my own family in the short time I've known you," I said. "Whatever happens, I'll always be grateful."

She clasped her hands to her heart, shaking her head, tears in her blue eyes. "Mahalia didn't deserve you, dear." Gordon turned away from me suddenly, a flicker of magic forming over her desk. "I have a meeting with South America," she said. "I'll let you know as soon as I hear."

I exited her office, and though innocuous in fact, the door closing behind me sounding far less like wood on wood and much more like the final bell that marked my doom.

CHAPTER FIFTEEN

I almost went back to my room but the thought of remaining inside, enclosed and trapped, made me feel like an animal in a cage. How many times could I walk the grounds of the Yard in twenty-four hours? Many, and enough to make myself a bit mad. I considered a trip to Annenberg Hall for breakfast though my stomach churned with anxiety and hunger nowhere to be found. Maybe the act of eating would distract? Then again, I'd be forced to face the stares, the whispers and the steady and constant reminder that I did not belong, would never belong and might find myself in this state for the rest of my life.

I'm certain you're as tired of my whining and

complaining as I was by now. No matter how firmly I took myself in hand, however, I couldn't seem to shake off the weight of this cloud of misery that pushed against my shoulders and dropped my gaze to the ground in front of me. I longed so much to reach out to Sassafras, to speak to someone who knew and understood me. I'd told him to stay behind, to take care of my sister, but I wanted him to take care of me now so badly I caught myself from calling his name in my head just as fate intervened.

Varity Rhodes appeared as if by magic, no pun intended, planting herself in my path with that crooked grin and authentic kindness radiating from her, just enough of a distraction to save Sassafras from the guilt I knew he would endure—already did, truth be told—if I exposed my misery and fear I'd made the worst possible choice by accepting Mahalia's orders without fighting for my place in the coven.

"You're still here." She seemed delighted to see me, though her smile quickly faded to concern. "Did you hear back from the other school?"

I nodded, doing my best to keep my reserve. "Apparently, I'm not welcome."

She didn't hold back her anger, had no concern showing her own emotions. "Idiots," she said.

Then paused, shaking her head. "What are you going to do?"

"Gordon is still checking with other territories." I felt restlessness force me forward and Varity fell in beside me as I carried on, though it was she who guided our direction and I did nothing to shift that path, finding having a companion made the idea of going to the dining hall much more appealing. How strange that having someone at my side increased my confidence so very much. I'd never needed such support. Then again, I'd always had Sassafras.

He'd be miffed to think I'd replaced him so easily.

Feeling better was definitely a bonus. And had me thinking about Demetrius all over again. I shared my encounter from the morning with my new friend if only for something to share, though I held off confessing my few moments of weakness falling under the spell of the Dumont she warned me against. Varity listened carefully and paused near the entry to the hall to let me finish before she spoke herself.

"Come with me." She spun and marched off, leading me away from food—that my stomach now grumbled over—not stopping until we reached the chapel. This time, however, she didn't stop behind the oak but out in the open, where Demetrius had entered and exited the Stronghold. "I want to help," she said. And waved at the air, blue flame waking. The portal opened at her command while my heart sped up, the sight of the stone wall on the other side luring me closer. But Varity stopped me before I could pass through. "It won't let you," she said. "You have to be an Enforcer or in the program."

"We don't know that for sure," I said. "And I have sorcery." If I was right about Demetrius and his companions, this might prove that the dark power I carried made passing the Stronghold's wards a possibility.

"I won't break the law," Varity said then, firm and without threat or anger. As genuine as she was with me, she seemed to carry that authenticity to every part of her. I may have grumbled internally, with Burdie doing the same along with me, but I understood and respected my friend's commitment. "But I can go have a look around myself." She gestured at the portal. "Let me feel what you felt."

I wasn't sure she would even be able to, since I sensed no sorcery in her, but it was worth a try. It was quickly apparent she couldn't, however, though I finally managed to connect with her witch magic and let it sense the darkness that was the blossom beneath me.

"Got it," she gasped a little. "Good gracious, that's... something." She'd gone a bit pale but grinned a shaking grin before waving. "Hang on, I'll be right back." And, with that, she stepped through and vanished, the portal closing behind her.

Leaving me to stand in some frustration and discomfort at the corner of the chapel in the morning sunlight and wait. Like a good little witch. Something I was not.

At least, not anymore.

"Good morning, Ethpeal." I looked up to find Odette Dumont approaching, her sister, Naudia at her heels, the slight young man trailing behind the younger Dumont barely registering power. She'd called him Ralph, hadn't she? Odette, however, radiated it, a sun shining brightly and glaringly, as though she poured power into her aura as proof of her magic. Surely, I was reading more into her brightly glowing self, that my grumpiness and return to dissatisfaction with my predicament was making me sullen about others in possession of what I'd lost. She certainly didn't seem to be aggressive about it, even if her sister and Ralph both looked down at me with what seemed to be disdain. Odette's lovely face was all smiles, her magic reaching out to mine, hourglass body perfection in her pink twinset and pencil skirt, hair a cascade of shining blonde curls. I felt frumpy in her presence, knowing I'd done little to make myself physically appealing, more focused on my circumstance than how I looked today. Not that it mattered, but feeling badly about myself seemed to be a trend and I would have preferred it not be an issue.

"Good morning," I said, nodding to Naudia and Ralph before refocusing on Odette.

"I heard about Europe." The elder offered a pouting moue with her bow lips. "Mummy contacted me this morning. What a terrible situation you find yourself in. Lund should be ashamed of such petty behavior."

"I'm sure she believes she's justified," I said, not wanting to have this conversation with the gorgeous and powerful witch I wished would just walk away, please, and leave me alone. I didn't entirely trust her motives, and felt nothing of real concern in her, after all. If anything, she barely contained her curiosity, and I knew the moment she walked away she'd be gossiping about me to whoever crossed her path. Not that I blamed her, but I wasn't about to pour my heart out to someone like her.

"Well, I think it's a waste of talent, and so does Mummy." She shook her head, still pouting.

"That's kind of you to say," I said. "It was nice to meet you. I wish you the best in your time here."

"And you, dear Ethpeal." Her pout vanished instantly, traded for a fake smile.

"Please, tell Ivan thank you for his kindness." I hadn't meant to prod her, I swear. In fact, I have no idea why I blurted that request to her just as she was about to move off. It caught her attention like nothing else, even Naudia and Ralph freezing in place and finally looking my way. What had I said? My sudden nervousness had me carrying on while Odette's blue eyes watched with intensity that had me wishing I hadn't said a word. "He was one of the only people here to treat me like a person." Implying she hadn't? Ethpeal, stop talking. But I couldn't, the elements help me, I simply couldn't make my lips stop moving. "It was so lovely to just walk and talk and not think about anything. He's very funny." Dear stars and spells, what was wrong with me? I watched her face tighten, her smile gone rigid as I went on like a rambling fool, felt her power intensify, hyperfocus on me, while I finally ground to an awkward and horrific halt. "I've never met anyone like him."

I was blushing. And there was something

seriously wrong with me.

Odette finally blinked, though not before I registered the flaring jealousy that crossed her face, the way her entire being flinched at my final words. She seemed to shake free of that reaction, however, letting out a tinkling laugh and wiggling the fingers of one hand in my direction.

"I'm sure I will," she said. "Safe travels, Ethpeal." As she walked off, I couldn't help but imagine her voice add, *and good riddance.*

I was obviously in the midst of losing my mind. I would never have allowed myself such a ridiculous bout of blathering a mere few days before now. How had I so utterly lost my ability to be a rational and reasonable person, fallen into a whirlpool of disaster, self-sabotage and inappropriateness?

I really needed to leave this place.

ETHPEAL HAYLE. I winced at Lund's contact. The witch had one volume, apparently, at least when it came to me. *MY OFFICE, NOW.*

What had I done this time? At least the summons silenced my internal cringing and stoked my anger all over again. For the first time, I felt gratitude toward the Headmistress, which meant I didn't hesitate as I turned and headed to Massachusetts Hall.

Chapter Sixteen

I once again stood in the Headmistress' office, for the third time in less than a day, only remembering as I stopped with my shoulders back and my jaw set that I'd left Varity behind in the Stronghold and hadn't informed her of what was going on.

Considering I had no idea if I could even reach her where she'd gone, I let the situation be and instead gave the head of Coven Hall my full attention.

This was the first time I confronted her without backup, I realized, no Di Gordon to make her behave, no Gilleland or Carista to speak for me. It was obvious she'd arranged this meeting that way on purpose, her power blocking the door when I entered and sequestering the both of us from the outside world.

It was also the first time I actually felt nervous she might do something untoward, her anger radiating from her in waves, the magic she commanded pushing against me as though it agreed completely with her opinion of my person. Not that I was afraid of her, not really. Instead, I hated that I felt even remotely intimidated and very carefully but firmly found myself pushing back.

She noticed immediately, dark eyes widening, fury overtaking her expression, though when she spoke it wasn't to berate me for standing my ground.

"I have had the displeasure," she spit at me, "of contact with your mother, Mahalia." She spoke that name like a curse, almost stumbling over it.

Why would she even attempt such contact? "I'm sorry to hear that." I hadn't meant to be facetious, but it came out before I could stop it.

Lund seemed startled by my offer of sarcastic sympathy, but it didn't alleviate her animosity at all. "At the suggestion of Council Leader Gordon," she went on, words grinding over her barely contained fury, "I made the request that you be reinstated in the Hayle coven so that you might attend this institution."

I'd forgotten that option had even been on the table and winced inwardly, though I refused to let Lund see it. "How unfortunate," I said.

"Indeed." She thudded one fist against her thigh before returning to her desk and seating herself carefully behind it, rigid and firmly under control. She'd clearly registered her spiral and had taken it in hand, but I had no doubt one false move from me would exacerbate the issue and return her to the edge of her anger. While I sympathized with her for her hatred toward my mother, I truly wished she would take a moment and try to see I wasn't Mahalia Hayle and never would be.

Too much to ask, sadly.

"Your *mother*," she had to stop a moment before going on, lips twisting, "has assured me you will not now, nor will you ever be, welcome in the Hayle coven again."

Her words hurt me far more than she would ever know. I finally found my lifelong poise and dove deeply into it, wrapping my need to hide my feelings and my pain from those around me like the strongest wards, the warmest cloak. Lund would not have the satisfaction of knowing how deeply she'd cut me.

Because despite everything, a tiny part of me

hoped one day Mahalia might relent and let me come home. Silly, really. Childish, yes. But a remnant inside me I carried nonetheless, a remnant of the little girl who only wanted her mother's love and never, ever received it.

"I see." I nodded once, stiff and formal. "That's that, then."

"It is." Lund stood abruptly once more, pointing to the door. "I have done everything I could." Liar, and yet, she believed it, and who was I to argue. "I have gone above and beyond for you, Ethpeal Hayle, and neglected other students and their needs to do so." She clearly justified her actions to herself, though I saw through her immediately. Not that I could stop her from her final judgment. "Without a family to claim as your own, you are heretofore required to exit this campus and not return."

And that, as they say, was that.

I don't remember leaving her office, though I vaguely recall her magic boosting me through the door. In fact, I have no recollection of exiting Massachusetts Hall at all. I must have meandered, mind lost, heart broken, into the Yard, because when I finally did register where I was and what I was doing, I had found a tree to huddle beneath, tears tricking down my cheeks into my hands, while people passed me without so much as a glance in my direction.

It didn't take long for my silent weeping to run its course, though I did sit there for a long time, lost in thought and emotion, watching the world stride past me, giggling, chatting, sense of belonging something out there that I wasn't welcome to take part in. I'd never felt so detached from myself before, from the world around me, and I missed his presence until he took a seat next to me, the black blossom of his sorcery sliding over mine bringing me back to myself at last.

"I heard," he said.

"I'm sure everyone has by now." It was impossible to muster emotion, and I was grateful for that. I'd felt enough, thank you. I turned to him, squinting as the sunlight caught the corner of my eye, the scent of something fresh with a citrus base coming from his hair as a faint breeze passed over him to me. I noted the little flecks of silver in his eyes, the way the corners crinkled, his propensity for roundness of his cheeks and chin. The way his full lips bowed at the top, not a trace of the kind of heavy facial hair Ivan Dumont sported on the sorcerer's soft, tanned cheeks. He took my scrutiny without reaction aside from the kind expression he wore, which made me angry for some reason. "Are you going to tell me what you were up to? I've been through a lot, Demetrius," I cut off any protest with all the wry humor I could muster, though it wasn't much. "If you shut me down again, I might just cry on you."

He shrugged and grinned. "I wouldn't mind."

"*I* would," I said, stilted and cross without really feeling it, the turn to lightheartedness a boon, to be honest. "I'd hold it against you forever and ever."

"I might not look it," he said, eyes sparkling, "but I'm strong, Ethpeal. I can take it. You need a shoulder, I'm here." He sighed then. "Just don't ask me what's going on, please. I can't tell you anything."

"Are you in trouble?" It surprised me, really, how worry woke when I asked that question. So, I could feel after all, excellent. I hadn't lost my ability, it seemed, as much as I would have preferred otherwise. Still, the crippling emotionlessness that I knew had to simply be my mind's veil over the hurt I couldn't yet face wasn't serving me. Caring about someone else did. And yet, why was it I cared so much? I blamed it on my need for distraction even as he answered me.

"Not as much as you might think," he said in his cryptic fashion, "but enough to make life interesting." He sighed then, arms on his upraised knees, looking out over the Yard and letting peace settle over both of us. I didn't fight it, sinking into the oddly familiar feel of him, the way our sorcery interwove together beneath us like old friends reacquainting after a long separation. Was that it? The connection I felt to him? Only our magic, mine long without another of its kind to befriend? Possibly. Probably. And yet, as he leaned into me with one shoulder, casually familiar, I found myself wishing he'd put his arm around me and contemplating how soft his lips might feel on mine.

Until he turned his head and looked at me, smiling like he knew what I was thinking. That jerked me free of the strange sensation building between us and had me clearing my throat and sitting up straighter while the world returned in a rush of sound and people.

"Thank you for your concern," he said like I hadn't reacted at all.

"Idiot," I said. He had no idea I was talking to myself. I didn't get to tell him otherwise as Varity Rhodes approached, crouching in front of both of us, her eyebrows raised as she looked back and forth between us like we were the last two people she expected to see together. Considering I'd left her last in a subterfuge exploration of the Stronghold, seeking his reason for entering with the three strangers I'd seen, it was only fair she reacted that way.

"I couldn't find trace of them," she said, nodding to Demetrius, "or him, either. Whatever they were up to in the Stronghold, if he's not talking, we might have to *make* him."

I gaped at her, the gut-punch of her aggressive reveal undoing all the good this short respite in Demetrius' presence had lent me. He didn't react badly, he never seemed to, but his power retreated from me as we both absorbed what she'd said, and that connection severed itself in a gentle but final kind of way that had me wishing Varity hadn't found us at all.

That I'd minded my own business.

"Good luck, Ethpeal," Demetrius said, standing and brushing the seat of his jeans off with both hands. "I hope you find your path, wherever it leads you." He walked away while I could only sit there and watch him go, wishing he'd come back.

Chapter Seventeen

Varity took his place, scooting in next to me, arms hugging her knees. "We're not going after him?"

I shook my head, leaning back against the tree. "It's just a wild goose chase," I said, knowing I sounded defeated but not sure how else to be. "I'm sorry to have dragged you into it. This has nothing to do with me." I fought off Burdie's grumbling, speaking to her echo as much as to Varity. "Whatever Demetrius is up to, it's his business."

If only I believed that.

Varity huffed a little. "I don't know you well yet," she said, "but I get the feeling you don't quit easily."

I know she didn't mean that harshly. In fact, I had the impression Varity was a clear-spoken and honest person who didn't believe in filtering what she said or how she felt, and I admired her for that. The trouble was her attitude was only making my present situation worse.

"I don't have a choice." I told her about Lund and my mother's final word.

Varity's frown deepened until I was done. "Wait, repeat that for me?"

What did she want, a written statement? "I'm covenless. Without Mahalia's support, I can't enroll." Why was she beating me over the head with the details when she already knew them? This wasn't the first time I'd told her so. Or was it? I'd been living this nightmare for a short period of time, but it felt like forever and that everyone I knew was up to speed.

Varity perked suddenly, laughed a sharp bark of a sound, and grabbed my hand. When she leaped to her feet, hauling on me, I joined her, startled and a little annoyed at being witchhandled that way. But her good humor was infectious to the point I felt my unease and unhappiness dissipating even if only because it was impossible to remain in the doldrums with her looking at me with that goofy smile of hers.

"Come on," she said for the second time that morning, pulling me along with her yet again on another crazy adventure, no doubt, and one that would likely end in yet more failure and disappointment. I was just pliable enough in my weakness, however, to follow along anyway, even if only to distract myself a little longer.

Because when I finally did come back to reality, I'd be leaving Harvard Yard, Coven Hall and everything else behind me for parts unknown and I just wasn't ready to do that yet.

I hadn't expected to end up at University Hall, nor to be led past my quarters, the office of the leader and almost to the end of the corridor. That's why I stood, gaping a little and without comprehension, as Varity first knocked and then swiftly entered the door into the room beyond. I followed with some trepidation, noting the young witch at the desk on the other side at least smiled in greeting as Varity entered and, a moment later, let us both into the room past her desk where an older witch sat writing at a desk similar to the one Di Gordon used.

When she glanced up, I noted the familial similarity immediately, wondering if all Rhodes witches looked alike, age difference or not, while she stood and circled to embrace Varity.

"Auntie Vespa," my friend said. Another "V" name. Was it a Rhodes tradition? I was going to lose track of them in short order if so.

"Varity, my dear," the witch said as I realized who we now talked with. She had to be the Rhodes representative on the NAWC. She turned to me then, those same pale blue eyes taking me in, though without the dislike I'd seen from Violet and Lund, though the fondness of Di Gordon and the professors absent. It was obvious to me she studied me with some clinical detachment, and I was actually grateful for her distance. "You must be Ethpeal," she said.

I was surprised by her offer of power and reciprocated quickly, nodding. "Council Member Rhodes," I said.

"I was hoping for a chance to meet you before you left us." I wasn't sure if she really meant it considering I'd been here for a full day, staying in the Council hall, without a peep from her or any other family. Then again, I'd been wandering a great deal, so I chose to give her the benefit of the doubt.

"My departure," I said, "is imminent."

"So I've heard." She gestured for the two of us to join her on the love seats in the far corner of her office, dark walls engulfing us, the curtains drawn across her towering windows, a grimly observant ancestress staring at me from a portrait across the room. The heavy scent of roses had my nose twitching. "A most unfortunate affair. I do wish there was something we could do."

Again, I chose to believe the sentiment. But when she finished, Varity clearly took her at her word where I might not have entirely.

"We can, Auntie," my friend said, almost bubbling over in excitement.

"Do tell." Vespa's smile was clearly doting and her tone just a little condescending, enough I assumed she loved her niece but didn't exactly expect great things from her.

Varity didn't seem to notice, beaming at me. "We could invite Ethpeal to join the Rhodes family."

They could... *what?*

Vespa seemed as taken aback as I was, though she recovered far more quickly than I had, chuckling at what had to be a shocked expression on my face.

"I take it my dear Varity didn't tell you her intentions," she said, patting her niece's knee with a little sigh, though she didn't say no right away. Instead, she leaned back into the sofa with a growing look of curiosity and debate that gave me time to process the idea and then begin waffling.

Did I want to join another family? Burdie roared her response as loudly as if Lund had summoned me with a no that reverberated through my mind. But Thaddea quickly smothered her protest, softly and kindly supporting me while whispering to her fellow echo until my great-grandmother's protests waned and faded.

Leaving me to myself and my own mixed feelings while Vespa spoke.

"You know," she said, sounding mildly surprised and almost amused, "I hadn't considered it. Not even for a moment. The thought did not occur to me. How brilliant you are, Varity." The girl beamed at her aunt, and I wondered how often Varity was overlooked and underestimated. Because of her sister, Violet? Possibly, and probably. A fierce protectiveness and sense of possession engulfed me when I met Varity's eyes and I knew from that moment on, no matter where life took me, no matter what happened to me, Varity Rhodes would have my support and be my friend until the day we died.

And probably beyond.

It was that sudden surge of emotion that buoyed me while I spoke. "Is it a possibility?" My reservations faded in the wake of understanding.

Not only could I join Coven Hall, were I accepted, I could thumb my nose at Lund while making my mother furious.

Three wins in one choice? *What* reservations?

"What a coup," Vespa said with a sly smile for both of us, doing nothing to hide her own machinations. I grinned back, shakily, while she laughed and stood, pacing the room a little with her hands behind her back, radiating mischief. "It would certainly enrage a certain witch we both dislike." Did she mean Lund or my mother? It didn't matter. "Knocking the wind out of Mahalia Hayle would be a first for anyone," she said, choosing the witch she meant. "That idea pleases me very much." Again she laughed, short and edged, but with an amusement that belied her intent.

"So, we can do it?" Varity almost bounced on her seat while I held myself still and quiet just in case.

Just in case.

But Vespa seemed determined despite my nervous unwillingness to allow this hope to take the place of the previous.

"I think we can," she said. "Ethpeal, if my sister, our leader, is amenable, how would you like to join the Rhodes coven?"

CHAPTER EIGHTEEN

Council Leader Di Gordon didn't act surprised when we all landed in her office, so I assumed Vespa warned her during our short walk between doorways. If anything, she seemed delighted and first hugged the Rhodes Council member before turning to me with a hopeful smile.

"You said yes, I take it?"

I nodded immediately, Varity now hugging my arm with her own, linking us together, my soon-to-be sister in magic vibrating her excitement. What I wasn't expecting was for the door to open yet again and Violet to stride through, scowling at Varity and myself, before ignoring the Council Leader in favor of turning on her aunt.

"Have you lost your mind, Auntie?" The lack of respect Violet showed her superior had me gaping. Anyone who tried to speak to my mother that way would have found themselves on the floor, gasping for air and minus most of their own personal magic for good measure.

Vespa simply rolled her eyes at her niece and shrugged. "Hush, child," she said. "The choice is made. I've already reached out to your mother, and she's agreed."

Violet spluttered before reining herself in. "I'll contact her right now," she said, shooting me a glare while understanding ricocheted inside me.

"You are heir," I blurted.

"Of course, I am," Violet shot at me. "And there's no way I'm accepting you into our coven without very good reason." She shuddered a bit dramatically, in my opinion. "It's bad enough you're a *Hayle*," she said so spitefully I felt my anger surge, "but attracting the animosity of *that witch*," Violet let out a huff, "is absolutely the very end."

My decision to say yes was starting to wane. "I won't go where I'm unwanted."

Vespa's power snapped against Violet, bouncing off Varity, which meant I felt it, too. "Enough," she said, her substantial magic smothering the coven's heir and her protests. "You might be next in line, but you're not leader yet, Violet. Speak to your mother, by all means. I'll be sure to do the same. She will know her oldest daughter treated her elder with such disrespect while undermining a new member to our family."

Violet paled, bowed her head, though I could tell she wasn't done yet. "I'm sorry, Auntie," she said. "You know I only have our family's safety in mind."

"I do." Vespa softened again, nodding to me. "However, I do believe, as does your coven leader, that welcoming such a powerful witch and magic user of other abilities into our fold, one who will no doubt make a name for herself in the ranks of the Enforcer order, no less,"—wait, was that pride in her voice? For *me*?—"could only be of benefit for our family."

Violet hesitated a very long moment. "How do we know she's powerful?" Even she seemed to realize her question was obtuse and out of line because she twitched after asking it.

Vespa had already tested me, moments before, in her office. A quick and yet thorough examination I'd borne quietly and without hiding anything from her which led to a frank conversation that immediately preceded her convincing her coven leader to welcome me to the family.

"Ethpeal bears a sizable personal power source," Vespa said—yes, that was *pride*, imagine that. I'd explained it was Sassafras and his meddling as full disclosure, but she hadn't seemed to care. "Not to mention Fey blood and power, and sorcery." Vespa clasped her hands under her chin. "So much ability. We simply cannot allow such a powerful and talented young witch to fall by the wayside. The Rhodes family is delighted to welcome you into our hearts and our magic, Ethpeal. Isn't that right, Violet?"

Her tone might have been kind, but her magic allowed no argument. Still, the family's heir paused one last breath before nodding again and backing off at last.

I'd have trouble with her. No doubt she feared I might usurp her position or try to. I could see her fear in her eyes, her suspicion and doubt. Family politics, my old nemesis. I'd once expected to bear the weight of such on my shoulders. Instead, I'd been freed from such a life. Violet could have it.

Better, this, at least, I was familiar with and decided then and there to nip her worry in the bud.

"I'm grateful for the chance to be a Rhodes," I said, "and do justice to the name and coven. My decision to become an Enforcer stands, however.

Which means I'll be divesting myself of the family power when the time comes." Was I really going to be an Enforcer after all? Was this even happening for real? I caught my breath as I went on. "But I will bear allegiance and connection to my new family all the days of my life and I will not forsake you."

Violet seemed to absorb what I said. Her power retreated, her concern lessened, though I had no doubt she still worried. Whatever her fears, I did my best to contain my now soaring heart because what she thought didn't matter to me even a little bit.

I was going to be an *Enforcer,* and nothing made me happier.

"You don't need my official approval," Gordon said, "but consider it granted." She beamed at me, laughing as I felt myself sag a little in Varity's grasp, gratitude and relief washing over me, tears in my eyes as I laughed in return.

Mahalia would be absolutely livid. I wished I'd be there to see her lose her mind. But I had one witch who hated me who I would get to witness eat crow and I simply couldn't wait to tell Headmistress Kirstin Lund I was a Rhodes witch.

Roundabout or not, my plan was now in play.

CHAPTER NINETEEN

"When you're ready," Professor Lisa Noe-Bradford said, stepping outside the pentagram she'd created with her Enforcer power, "you may begin."

I drew a short breath and nodded, reaching for the magic inside me while the power she'd contained me in rose to greet me. Even as my mind spun, struggling for focus, because how was it I suddenly stood in the massive entry space to the Stronghold, surrounded by Enforcers, the Council Leader, my new Rhodes family-to-be and other curiosity seekers when just a short time ago I was certain I would never be admitted to this exalted order?

Not that I was a Rhodes until their leader finalized my welcome. There was no sign in the Enforcer teacher's face that Professors Gilleland and Carista had spoken to her about my fears, so I set that conundrum aside in favor of this very important moment. Whatever Demetrius was up to, I now had a chance to uncover it in my own time, not in the spare I had while hanging in limbo between possible futures.

I pulled myself back from the memory of being led to Lund's office by Vespa Rhodes, Varity striding at my side, unable to wipe the grin from her face, witness to that member of Council's firm and commanding dealings with the furious Headmistress.

"Ethpeal Hayle," she'd told the spluttering Lund, "will be admitted and tested for Enforcer eligibility as a pending member of our coven."

"She's not a member yet," Lund managed.

"A technicality," Vespa insisted, bulldozing over the other witch's protests while Gordon backed her up, bless her.

"Vonda Rhodes herself will arrive tomorrow," the Council Leader said, "to formalize Ethpeal's addition to her coven. For now, it's expeditious to allow her to be tested for assignment to Enforcer training while we wait for that leader to arrive."

Lund tried to fight, but with the commanding and insistent pair of witches bullying her into compliance, she had no options.

"Very well," she'd finally snarled. "But when this falls apart and she shows her true colors, the guilt be on both of you."

Child. The massive presence of the Stronghold slid over my mind, startling me as much now as it had the moment that I'd passed through the portal Varity quickly dragged me to as soon as we departed Lund's office. *You are unsettled.*

My apologies, I sent back, the pressure of its mind—could I call it a mind?—not so much a weight as it was a limitless mass of nothing and everything all at once I found disconcerting but stirred giddy excitement in me regardless.

None necessary, it responded with that ponderous and awe-inspiring depth of measure. *I have no doubt you will find a place of prominence here, Ethpeal Hayle.*

Its confidence in me helped shift my thoughts from the whirlwind of how to now and settled my mind as I'd been unable to do on my own.

Thank you, I sent as I expanded my chest with a full breath this time and settled into myself. No longer did the staring eyes of the gathering bring me self-consciousness or concern. All that mattered was the rising blue flame and the humming pulse of its power as I easily tapped into it and tied myself to it with the magic that I carried inside me.

The flames instantly reacted, flaring in a dance of joy that I felt to the very core of my soul, my lips parting in a grin, electric goosebumps arching across the surface of my skin while a bubble of giddy laughter emerged from me, unbidden and uncontrolled. I found myself spinning in a circle in utter delight, drawing the flames to me to undulate across my hands, through my fingers like a beloved pet fawning over my touch. The magic of the Enforcer order wriggled in pleasure as our powers met, my sorcery blossoming fully, the Fey energy flaring in green sparks through those flames like tiny, flittering fairies making merry in the waves of blue. There was a brief instant when I felt something connect to me, something familiar, a face flashing in my mind that held for the barest second, hardly long enough for me to identify her. And then a giant surge of what I can only name as ecstasy carried my heart upward, my arms rising of their own accord as the blue fire engulfed me fully before sinking again to pool at my feet, circling slowly, almost languid as it finally absorbed into my own magic and flared once before settling firmly into place.

No one said a word for a long moment, long enough for me to come back to myself, still smiling, body vibrating with the experience I'd just embraced, until I realized there was something wrong, if the gaping stares I now registered were proof of issue.

It wasn't until Council Leader Gordon stepped forward, hands clasped to her heart, I understood my panic wasn't needed and nothing was wrong, exactly. Her sudden smile shattered the frozen moment of shock and freed everyone else as she hurried to me and took my hands in hers, tears standing in her eyes. I caught the murmurs of surprise from those who observed as Gordon pulled me in for a hard, happy hug.

"Well done, Ethpeal." I'd never experienced such fierce pride before, mirrored almost immediately by Vespa Rhodes who pulled me out of Gordon's grip only to embrace me herself.

"Your family is so proud of you." She let me go, cackling and trembling just a little, absolutely wicked smile lighting her face with pure delight. "Aren't you just a wonder?"

I had no idea why they were so excited. "I did all right, then," I said.

"More than all right." That was Noe-Bradford, the head of Enforcer training joining us with a gentle smile, eyes lit with amusement. "I've never witnessed such an event. Our power didn't just accept you, Ethpeal. It bonded you to us forever."

It wasn't hard to find looks of jealousy in the gathered watchers, some of the students and even full Enforcers doing nothing to mask their envy. So, I hadn't made friends, it seemed. Though I did note Ivan Dumont's speculative look and the way Demetrius Strong, lingering next to Jeffery on the periphery of the crowd, grinned at me with a double thumbs up so enthusiastic I grinned back despite myself.

"The moment Raoul returns, we must introduce you." Vespa's breathless excitement hadn't faded. "Our Enforcer Leader will want to greet you personally."

"I've already informed Leader Donovan," Gordon said. "As soon as he's completed his present mission, he'll be back to confirm Ethpeal's assignment to training. For now, however, I think it's safe to say it's time you retrieved your things, my dear, and took your quarters here at the Stronghold where you belong."

Someone muttered something in fury, but I didn't bother looking Lund's way as the stomping and angry Headmistress stormed off, a portal hastily opened to allow her to exit. Whatever her opinion of me, it seemed my fate was now out of her hands. While I was likely in for an uncomfortable three years if she had any say in the matter, the truth—only now sinking in—was more than sufficient to smother any concern her continuing hatred might have had.

Even she couldn't ruin this moment for me. In fact, nothing could.

CHAPTER TWENTY

Varity bounced onto my bed while I began to unpack, laying back on my pillow with her hands behind her head. She hadn't stopped smiling since she'd volunteered to help me retrieve my possessions and insisted that I be her roommate. I hadn't argued, happy for the company and the friendship, as unfamiliar as that feeling was. Still riding the high of my test, I couldn't help but share her optimism as she carried on the conversation she'd begun the moment we were alone.

"Mother's going to adore you," she said, repeating herself for the fifth time. "Everyone will." Did she know I needed reassurance after the family I'd come from? Yes, the Hayle coven loved me, I had no doubt of that, but there was too much fear, an underlying anxiety in my old family that made truly accepting that love an impossibility. One misstep would easily lead to punishment and, proof in the pudding, even banishment, so this whole experience with the Rhodes coven and my now bright and shining future really needed reinforcement.

I was still pinching myself.

"Thank you, Varity." I paused in my unpacking to sit next to her, the stone walls of our room gray and dull in appearance but the most beautiful space I'd ever seen. The narrow slit of a window showed a cloudy sky devoid of sunlight but gave me a sense of welcome and connection I'd never known. Maybe it was the steady and supportive presence of the Stronghold's massive mind or the simmering blue fire I now carried inside me, but whatever the case, I had never been so calm and at peace with myself. "Without you, I don't know what would have happened to me."

"You'd have made something of yourself no matter what." She sat up and hugged me quickly, letting me go in a rush that left me a bit off balance. "I knew it the moment we met." She let out a long and satisfied sigh. "How did it feel?"

"How did what feel?" I rose and went back to

placing my possessions in the tall, wooden wardrobe at the end of my bed, tucking my shoes neatly into the bottom of the tall space.

"When the fire took you like that." She didn't lie back again, arms around her knees, a bit of awe in her voice.

"I don't know how to describe it." I paused with a sweater in my hands, the softness of it suddenly heavy in my grasp as I turned to face her. "Like coming home, I suppose. Finding a part of me I never knew was missing." Guilt washed through me. "Was I really that unusual?" I'd already accepted there would be those who judged me, but how bad was it going to be, really?

She nodded immediately, without a trace of jealousy. "You were a shining blue star," she said. "I've never seen anything so amazing. When the fire came to my power, it just linked with me, you know?" I didn't, but I nodded anyway. "You? It consumed you. I was kind of worried about you, at first, truth be told. But you were smiling, Ethpeal, fit to split your face in two." She laughed then, tossing her hands before standing abruptly. "And the whole chamber sang, like the Stronghold itself rang a bell to say, 'Look! Here is Ethpeal Hayle, and she is mine now.'"

You are, that massive mind whispered in

response.

That made me laugh. "It agrees with you."

She blinked, smile fading, head tilting to one side. "What does?"

"The Stronghold." I waited for understanding to rise in her eyes, but she only shared puzzled curiosity. "It doesn't speak to you?"

Varity inhaled sharply then shook her head. Which had me instantly guilty and then stammering.

"I'm not crazy," I said.

She came to me, hands clasping my upper arms, my sweater still between us in my outstretched fingers. "I've heard it's possible," she said, low and quiet. "Rumors of this place having a soul." She shivered a little. "I believe you, Ethpeal, but I don't know I'd share with anyone else."

"Why?" I knew the answer, of course, but needed her to say it.

"You're already in for a time, I'm afraid." Varity let me go, turning to her own bed across the room, sinking into it. "Daughter of the Hayles, brought on by Rhodes without question, possessing so much magic outside a coven and now this." She waved at me, at the room around me, as though engulfing everything I'd gone through in the last little while with one gesture. "If they find out you can hear the Stronghold itself when not even the Enforcer leader can do so…"

I turned away, tucking my sweater onto a shelf and closing the doors with both hands before speaking. "I never asked for this." To belong, to be an Enforcer, yes, of course. But not to stand out. I'd lived my entire life doing my best for everyone else in an impossible situation that ended badly for me and my whole family. All I wanted now was to start fresh. It sounded like I might have stepped out of the magical frying pan and into the Enforcer fire.

"Hey!" She lunged to her feet, spinning me around, grinning all over again. "None of that. You're home, Ethpeal. You're where you belong. And don't let anyone get you down. Not even me." She rolled her eyes at me, sticking her tongue out and making me laugh before tugging me toward the door. "All they need is to meet you anyway," she said. "I know you'll fit right in."

We'd see about that.

We barely exited into the hallway, my new reluctance tempered by her infectious good nature, when a familiar pair made us pause. Demetrius didn't hesitate to hug me, letting me go after a solid moment of contact that had our sorcery entwining despite his recent retreat. The Enforcer power we now shared joined in, adding an extra layer to the contact that had me rather breathless despite the short duration of his embrace.

If he noticed, he didn't say, though there was a brightness to his cheeks and a light in his eyes that told me he likely knew exactly what I was feeling. "Well done, Ethpeal." He laughed a little, prodding Jeffery who grinned at me with a sheepish expression. "I told him you would pass with flying colors."

"Welcome to the order," Jeffery said, holding out one hand with his power floating around it. Whatever reservations he'd had about me had clearly been washed away by my admission to the Enforcer training program and though I could have held a grudge, it was obvious to me Jeffery's intent had been to protect Demetrius. Considering the feelings I was only beginning to adjust to—even as they expanded and prodded me for attention—I understood his heartfelt concerns completely and immediately returned his offer of power with my own.

"Thank you," I said, heart now almost bursting as I let the truth settle around me fully. "I'm really here, aren't I?"

Both young men laughed, Varity joining them, while I waffled between falling completely into maniacal giggles, hysteria a reaction I wasn't expecting, and the poise and containment I was used to. I settled on laughing with them because my heart simply wouldn't allow anything less.

"Let's show you around," Demetrius said.

"Food first." Jeffery groaned, rubbing his stomach while I realized it was likely around noon and I hadn't had breakfast.

"Yes, please," I said.

We were a merry band who strode the halls of the Stronghold, buoyed by each other and the camaraderie of our shared magic. This, I realized as we passed through the large opening to the entry hall of the massive fortress, was how family was supposed to feel. Not judging or wary or waiting for disaster to strike and tempers to heat, but easy, flowing and filled with possibility.

That feeling spluttered when we entered the hall, silence falling as everyone turned to stare. I hesitated only a moment, even as the deep and powerful voice of the Stronghold reached out to me.

You are one of them, it sent. *Show them and they will follow you anywhere.*

I acted on impulse, opening my power to everyone in the room. From the look Varity gave me, the shock that turned to excitement in her eyes, following that advice was exactly the right thing to do. She instantly opened her own Enforcer magic, Demetrius and Jeffery following right after. As I stood there on the threshold of the entry hall, I felt the wave of blue flame spark and then ignite through everyone within. From the collective of trainees and the few full Enforcers assembled, all the way to the root of the power that formed our order into the depths of the Stronghold, I experienced the complete embrace of not only the fire that connected us but the welcome and then connection of each and every soul in the room.

We glowed. I cannot describe it any better than that, the moment in time when our power all came together as one. That fiery star Varity mentioned, how she witnessed my joining to the power of the Enforcer order, passed from me to everyone present. It was almost as though we collectively inhaled and exhaled, the flames stoked so bright by our bonded magic that I felt briefly blinded by it. As it faded and retreated, but never completely died, I blinked through the sparks lingering in my vision while feeling, in a rush that left me wavering, the outpouring of the collective embrace and goodwill from all assembled.

Gone was their jealousy, their concern. Instead, I found myself waving and smiling back somewhat shyly at the enthusiasm of my welcome. Wrapped up in the warmth of the moment, everyone went back to their conversations and their private existence though I knew without a doubt in my mind what we'd all just experienced would tie us together for the rest of our lives.

How remarkable.

Ivan Dumont approached with a grin and a hug of his own. I accepted his embrace and was surprised to find he didn't affect me the way he had before. Yes, he was gorgeous still and his attention felt lovely, but my body's reaction was gone, the physiological need I'd felt passed and departed. I didn't miss it, however, much preferring the sense of peace I now possessed and could finally enjoy his company, to my surprise, without discomfort.

"You know how to make an entrance," he said, winking.

"She does at that." I turned from him at the sound of Noe-Bradford's voice, finding the Enforcer trainee professor smiling at me. She held out her hand, gesturing for me to join her, my friends—yes, my friends, and my family—heading for the portal and the Yard on the other side while I lingered at her request. "How are you feeling, Ethpeal?"

I almost told her about the Stronghold despite

Varity's suggestion otherwise but clamped down on that idea. Maybe I'd confess the truth to her at some point, but for now, I wanted to enjoy my new position as much as possible. "Amazing, professor," I said, hesitating then. Did I dare bring up my conversation with Gilleland and Carista?

"I'm glad to hear it," she said. "Professor Gilleland spoke with me earlier." I tensed, anticipating an uncomfortable conversation. "He has asked to be assigned as your mentor for your first year. Does that work for you?"

"Of course." I was delighted, in fact, though wondered why he hadn't said anything to her about what I'd seen. Maybe he had and they'd deemed it nonsensical. I found myself hesitating before speaking again. "And Professor Carista?" Because I'd come to adore them both, frankly, and hated to think I had to choose between them. Now that I was staying.

Now that I was *staying*.

Noe-Bradford laughed and nodded. "Trust me," she said, "Kate fought David for the assignment. I see no reason you can't have two mentors if they are amenable."

I smiled back at her. "Thank you, professor," I said.

"If you need anything," she said, stepping away,

"please don't hesitate. Class doesn't begin officially until the day after tomorrow, so you have time to settle in. I know Vonda Rhodes will want to spend some time with you when she arrives in the morning, so take the rest of today and adjust to being one of us." She hugged me again. "I'm so very happy for you, my dear," she whispered. But she pulled away quickly before I could respond and then strode off, leaving me to catch my breath and then pursue something to fill my empty stomach, though my heart was so very full.

Chapter Twenty-One

The Stronghold whispered a farewell to me as I passed through the portal and into the Yard on the other side, its presence almost wistful as I left it. I sent a cheeky salute in return, nearly floating as I linked arms with Varity and headed for Annenberg Hall. So strange, how quickly things could change. The last time I'd stood inside the dining space, I'd struggled with my sense of belonging, with wanting to fit in and yet keeping myself apart. This time, wrapped in the glow of that lingering magic we all shared, I found myself looking forward to everything to come, including putting myself in a position of social vulnerability.

Odette approached me, her simpering smile

tweaking my mood, though the sour look on Naudia's face and the way Ralph seemed to shrink back from me had me wondering if I really was ready to accept my place here entirely.

"Ethpeal!" Odette embraced me, to my surprise, her magic simmering around my new Enforcer power like a dog sniffing at a possible meal. There was nothing of the familial feeling I had from my fellow Enforcers in that contact, however, so I tried not to judge her for poking her magical nose in my business. "I just heard from Ivan. How wonderful for you. Though, honestly, had you been so desperately in need of a family to join, the Dumonts would have taken you in."

I gaped at her a moment, Varity's anger surging next to me.

"What's that supposed to mean?" My friend's animosity wasn't contained even a little, the tall Rhodes witch looming over the slight blonde with more than enough threat Odette should have thought twice about what she said next.

Which I suppose she did, and though she couched her following words in a softer and sweeter tone, her disdain wasn't lost on any of us. "Now, Varity, don't take it personally, but everyone knows the Dumont family is far more powerful than yours. I understand you haven't yet taken on the Rhodes power, Ethpeal. If you'd like I can speak to Mother about allowing you to join us if you'd prefer to accept magic that suits your station."

"I'd watch my tongue." I was surprised to find Violet Rhodes pushing her way through to confront the Dumont witch with a scowl on her face that aged her past her young years, giving me a brief glimpse into the witch she would become. "And my attitude."

"You can hardly argue the point, Violet," Odette said in a velvet voice and enough vitriol I wondered if the issue wasn't with me, but with the witch now standing in her way.

"I can," Varity's sister snapped, "and I will, any day. Is it time, Odette? Are you ready to put your magic where your mouth is?"

Interesting, though their mutual animosity had my attention and my power's as well.

"Oh, please," Odette said, waving one hand between them. "As if you are any match for me. You see, Ethpeal?" She arched a perfectly shaped eyebrow at me, tinkling laugh empty and sharp. "What you're saddling yourself with? Besides," she fixed Violet with a vicious look, "weren't you just saying how much you disagree with your mother's decision?"

Violet's jaw jumped. "Ethpeal is my sister now," she said with utter conviction that had me gaping, "as much as Varity is. And I will defend her as I would anyone in my coven."

"Not exactly yet," Odette said, malice in her sly smile.

From Violet's flat expression she was on the edge of rage. I'd seen such empty fury before and anticipated Odette ending up on her backside in short order. Instead, we were interrupted before a fight could break out, magical or otherwise.

"Odette." I hadn't noticed Ivan's arrival, though his anger was obvious, how his scowl radiated outward from him through his magic. I was tied to him now and that made it impossible not to sense his feelings, nor did he try to hide them from me as his disapproval pressed down on his cousin with the kind of weight that would have buckled a lesser witch to her knees.

Odette, for her part, took his admonishment with a pout and a pushback that did nothing to make him retreat. The flare of resentment that passed through her eyes wasn't aimed at him, however, but at me.

"Ah, well," she said then, brightening. "Whatever the path, the outcome is the same. How lovely for you, Ethpeal, to have found your place at last."

I murmured my thanks, slipping past her and her sister, Naudia's power brushing mine and, in that moment, I felt her insecurity, her nervousness and the fact she was afraid of me.

I hadn't been expecting that. Her whole attitude since we'd met had been one of outward disapproval and judgment. Feeling her fear, her anxiety in my presence, gave me a boost of confidence I wasn't proud of. I shouldn't have felt better knowing she perceived me as a threat. But somehow, having the younger Dumont sister on edge suggested to me perhaps Odette herself might have the same feelings and that pulled me out of the resentment her comments roused and into a place of power.

Beneath me? Likely. Still felt amazing, though.

"I'll make sure the Headmistress sends you your registration papers." I paused and turned back as Odette spoke again. Her smile was tight, going nowhere near her eyes, though she carried on as though we were the best of friends. "As her student assistant, and a fellow Dumont, I'm privy to all of her decisions." And now I knew how Odette had insider information that had nothing to do with Ivan. The fact Lund was a Dumont was news, however. Gordon had said her coven had been absorbed by another but hadn't told me which one. Funny, but that made me feel better, too. "I'll deliver them personally."

I nodded in agreement and carried on without another word, only wanting to escape her very uncomfortable presence. Ivan followed, tucking in behind me as Demetrius and Jeffery lunged for trays and plates of food, Varity lingering with me and keeping her eye on the Dumont Enforcer trainee while obviously wishing she could join our two friends in focusing on lunch.

"I'm sorry about Odette. She had no right to criticize another coven." The fact Ivan didn't address that to Varity had me frowning a little.

"I'm sure we can find it in our hearts to forgive her," I said. "Isn't that so, Varity?"

My tall friend snorted but shrugged. "If you say so, Eth."

Ivan inhaled as if he had more to say before stepping back. "Welcome to the order," he said. And turned and walked away while I fought off regret that I'd been short with him.

Even as I felt a surge of jealousy buffet my power, though when I turned and met Odette's eyes one last time, she was smiling all over again, no trace of that emotion visible in her expression or her magic.

CHAPTER TWENTY-TWO

The rest of the day seemed to go by in a haze of happiness I wasn't expecting and, when Varity suggested some selective debauchery, I immediately accepted. With a few other Enforcer trainees filling out our ranks and the streets of Boston wide open to us, we set out to wander from pool hall to bowling alley to café in search of fun.

The moment I set foot through the wards, I felt power snap in my mind.

ETHPEAL HAYLE. I was getting very tired of Lund yelling at me. *WHAT PART OF MY COMMAND DID YOU FAIL TO UNDERSTAND?*

I hadn't even considered the fact that I was still

under Yard restraint. I hesitated, Varity waiting with me, frowning as I shook my head at her in irritation. *Other students are allowed to leave the wards, Headmistress.*

OTHER STUDENTS, she sent, *ARE NOT ON PERMANENT PROBATION. REPORT TO ME AT ONCE.*

There was nothing to be done, though as I passed back through the barrier, Varity joining me, I waved her off.

"I'll deal with this," I said. "Go, have fun."

"I won't leave you," she said.

"She just wants to bully me further." There was no doubt of that in my mind, even as a thought crossed that had me grinning. "I won't be alone. Go, please. I'll feel better knowing one of us is enjoying ourselves."

Varity went, though with great reluctance, even as I headed back toward the Yard, pausing at a familiar door on my way.

Professor Gilleland answered this time and, when I told him where I was going and why, he immediately joined me. "Kate will meet us," he said.

Excellent. I had backup and was, for the first time, I felt, actually prepared for a confrontation with Headmistress Lund. She seemed surprised to find I wasn't alone this time, grumpy at the sight of both Gilleland and the panting but fully present Professor Carista who hurried in right behind us as we entered. She'd clearly come at a full run, cheeks pink from exertion, but there was nothing tired about her attitude as she planted herself at my side, Gilleland at the other, while Lund took in our united front.

"You broke the rule I set in place," Lund said. "Your provisional acceptance is now off the table."

She said it like it was the word and law. Wait, was she really going to do this?

"Headmistress," Gilleland said before I could let panic take me. "From what I understand, it's up to coven leaders of each family member to decide if they are permitted to leave Yard grounds during their time here at Coven Hall."

Lund looked like she would have happily murdered him on the spot if she thought she could get away with it. "Ethpeal Hayle doesn't have a leader," she said somewhat stiffly. If she beat that dead horse any more, it just might turn into a zombie and rise after all.

"She has been spoken for," Carista said as if Lund needed the reminder, testy tone not helping matters, though I was grateful for her irritation. "As you well know."

Lund's back stiffened. "Then let Vonda Rhodes present herself," she said. "Or remove this witch from my presence."

Like she had the power to just summon a coven leader. Gilleland hesitated while Carista spluttered.

"Very well," I said, interrupting all of them and making Lund stare. "One moment, please." And, knowing I was taking a huge leap of faith but trusting this was the time and place to call Lund's bluff before she somehow managed to follow through on her threat, I reached out through the tie I had to Varity and found the Rhodes magic. *Leader Rhodes*, I sent.

It took a moment for Vonda to answer, but when she did, I felt her contact, firm and confident, so strong in her control of her family power I caught a glimpse of her seated at a desk in a small room, writing something, sunlight pouring in over one shoulder.

Ethpeal, my dear. This was my first private contact with Vonda Rhodes, her warmth encouraging. *What do you need?*

Forgive me, I sent, *for the intrusion.*

Not at all. She sat back, smiling at me across the miles. *Congratulations are in order. I meant to reach out to you personally, but I wanted to give you time to appreciate your success. I hear you're going to make the kind of Enforcer that comes along only once every other generation.* The pride in her mental touch had me struggling against tears I didn't dare shed.

Thank you so much, leader, I sent. *Your faith in me means a great deal.*

This isn't a social call. I feel how troubled you are, she sent, setting her pen aside. *What's happening?*

I quickly showed her where I was and told her of Lund's demand.

Ridiculous, Vonda spluttered. *And utterly preposterous. Give me a moment.* I felt her magic expand and connect with me more fully, the reverberation of her mental voice echoing inside me as she spoke again. *What is the meaning of this?*

Lund actually swayed a little, but she didn't back down. "Leader Rhodes," she said out loud while Gilleland and Carista exchanged a smirk.

Headmistress. Vonda's tone cut sharply across Lund's words like a flaming sword. *I grow tired of hearing of your animosity and cruel treatment of a member of my family. Surely you have real work to do.*

"Ethpeal Hayle is not a Rhodes witch yet." Lund had certainly dug her heels into that fact, hadn't she? And seemed utterly unwilling to let it go.

A formality I chose to cement in person on the morrow, Vonda shot back. *Are you challenging my authority?*

"Not at all," Lund said. "Merely the facts."

Vonda's power rumbled like a rapidly approaching thunderstorm. *How dare you,* she snarled. *Interrupting my important tasks with your pettiness. The Council and the board of directors will hear of this outrage, make no mistake. I had planned a beautiful ceremony to welcome Ethpeal into our family. It would appear your selfishness means she won't get the kind of introduction to our coven she so deserves. My dear,* she addressed me directly, *my apologies, but we need to do this now. Are you ready?*

I opened my magic to her completely, feeling the faintest regret die as I smothered it. I wasn't a Hayle anymore and never would be again. Even Burdie and Thaddea, both of whom had been quiet since the Enforcer fire took up residence, didn't offer an argument.

"I'm ready, my leader," I said out loud for everyone's benefit.

Vonda's magic surged toward me, linking with me and filling me with the power of the Rhodes coven, taking me into the family with a sweeping warmth I would cherish for the rest of my days.

Or, at least, that was how I imagined it would go.

Except, it didn't, did it?

The instant the Rhodes magic touched mine, a giant spark of something I knew intimately, a power I'd spent my entire life with, surged at the connection point with a recoil that sent Vonda's magic back to her in a rippling wave that made us both gasp.

Even as my mother's voice, embedded in the power that rejected my new family, whispered, *Mine*.

CHAPTER TWENTY-THREE

Vonda tried again while I struggled to comprehend what was happening, the coven leader's not insubstantial power pushing hard against the barrier Mahalia had left behind. She tried cutting through it first, then penetrating it with a pointed attack. Battering it did nothing, nor did prying it open. When she finally retreated, her magic filled with sorrow and regret, I knew no matter what happened, I wouldn't be joining the Rhodes family after all.

My mother had seen to that.

I had no idea. I almost sobbed in my mind, fighting against Mahalia's lingering geas.

I'm so sorry, my dear. Vonda's disappointment

wasn't nearly as powerful as her compassion for me, a true testament to her heart and the magic of the Rhodes family. Bitter regret punched me hard in the chest, fury at my mother, desperate panic digging a giant hole in my confidence as I realized what this meant. *I wish I could help. But it appears there is nothing I can do unless your mother releases you.*

She banished me! I shouted that into the ether, though it did me no good.

She did, Vonda sent. *And, in cruelty, ensured you would never join another family ever again. Yet another reason to detest her.* She said that last as though to herself. *I wish you well, Ethpeal Hayle. But I'm afraid you're on your own.*

She retreated, leaving me shaking and bereft, Gilleland and Carista both staring at me in utter shock. Lund's soft crow of victory had me looking up in rage, burning in hateful fury, as she jabbed a finger in my direction, her other hand clutching, claw-like, at the front of her robe.

"I knew it!" She spit that at me as though she could poison me with her words, bring my end with her tone. "Foul creature, damaged and broken, you will never be a member of this institution, not for as long as I have breath!"

"Enough!" Di Gordon strode through the door,

slamming it open, Vespa Rhodes on her heels. I caught sight of the Council member's distress and realized she must have felt her sister's failed attempts to reach me and chose to bring Gordon to my defense. Though what the Council Leader could do for me from here I had no idea.

No one could help me. Would that I hadn't had this taste of my dream fulfilled.

Even as Gordon spoke. "I declare Ethpeal Hayle a ward of the Council," she said, "and as a ward, within her right to attend Coven Hall!"

Things were coming at me far too fast. I had just fallen into despair, only to have Gordon's appearance offer me a lifeline. Lund, for her part, seemed just as off-kilter, though she recovered fast enough, faster than me, at least.

"She's eighteen," she fired back. "Too old to be a ward."

"She's not eighteen for two more days," Gordon retorted with all the weight of the Council's power behind her, "and fully within rights to petition for guardianship." She turned to me then, eyes blazing, her hand outstretched. "Ethpeal, do you request such?"

"I do," I said, feeling the Council's power slam into me the moment I spoke the first syllable. My mother's geas attempted to block Gordon, but whether because I wasn't being joined to another family or out of the sheer brute force of Gordon's assault, it failed, the Council magic storming through Mahalia's attempt to control me and engulfing me in the full brunt of all of North America's combined power.

I gasped as it rushed through me, swallowing me. This was a totally different experience to the one I'd just gone through, the fire of the Enforcer order welcoming me and embracing me. This felt more like I was being devoured from the inside out and then the outside in again, dropping me into a bottomless well of magic that wanted to make me its own. I fought it, struggling to retain myself, the Enforcer fire surging forward to aid me, and, in short order, I emerged from the battle for control, still shaking but myself, at least.

I shook myself free in the middle of a screaming match, Lund and Gordon confronting one another in almost incoherent shouts, their magic sizzling around them. Gordon might have commanded all the power of North America, but Lund's magic was tied to ancient power that created Coven Hall and, from what I could tell, the pair were about equally matched, to my shock.

Lund finally backed down when I reached out to Gordon with my mind and magic intact. The

Headmistress seemed stunned the Council Leader's plan had worked, surely hoping I'd either collapse under the pressure, perhaps stripped by the Council's magic in its attempt to sever Mahalia's geas or that it, too, would fail and she'd be able to summarily kick me out once and for all. As it stood, she had to know she was beaten, Gordon retrieving the Council power and firmly reining it in, her mind reaching for mine as she spoke out loud.

"I've had enough of this." *Ethpeal, are you all right?* "Do not make me question your role as Headmistress of this institution further." *I had to do something. Did I hurt you?* "You're walking a fine line of insubordination to your Council Leader, Headmistress Lund, and I won't tolerate it any longer." *Please, tell me I didn't damage you.* That had a distinct tang of terror to it.

I'm fine, I sent back quickly then. *Thank you. I don't know* how *to thank you.*

She exhaled in my mind, her relief obvious. *I had to trust your power would protect you,* she sent, *and that of the Enforcers. I see I was right, though it was a close thing, no doubt. Desperate measures, my dear.* "Now, hand over Ethpeal's admission forms and stop this nonsense. You have an actual job to do, Kirstin, that has nothing to do with focusing on harassment of one student who did nothing to earn this treatment."

Lund still looked rebellious. "She's not a coven member." So stubborn, so hateful.

"Irrelevant," Vespa said, as calm as you please, as though she hadn't just borne witness to the amount of power the pair had thrown around. "As keeper of the laws for the NAWC, my word is binding and law. Do you debate that?"

Lund shook her head with sullen fury. "I do not," she said between clenched teeth. Finally, something she couldn't go against. Since she'd called upon law herself, after all.

Vonda waved one hand, a line of writing appearing before all of us that she read out loud. "Any foundling, covenless and adrift and not of their majority, may be made ward of the Council," she said.

Lund bobbed a nod. "I didn't argue that fact." She did, though. The way her throat worked, she realized her mistake as she blurted next, "Now that I know she's not yet eighteen."

Nice cover attempt, but weak, so weak. As weak as I now saw her, my panic and desperation broken, something inside me torn and irreparable, hate like I'd never felt aimed at her. I hoped she'd give me a reason at some point to challenge her. Whatever her reasons for despising me and my mother, she'd almost taken from me the future I knew was my destiny. The very thought of having to give up the Enforcer fire had me ready to fight the entire world if need be. Lund would find me a formidable adversary moving forward.

"Moreover," Vespa said, gesturing at the air, the original line of prose vanishing and a new one appearing, written in light and sparks but clearly readable, "any ward of the Council is deemed the responsibility of that Council and has all the rights and freedoms of any coven member."

Lund didn't comment.

"It is my judgment therefore," Vespa wrapped up with a smug smile, "that Ethpeal Hayle, as a ward of the Council, is entitled to entry into Coven Hall and the Enforcer order as she was made said ward prior to her eighteenth birthday."

"As soon as she passes that date," Lund grated through clenched teeth, "she no longer qualifies."

"Not so," Vonda said, almost gleeful as she gestured, one last bit of writing flaring to life, almost impacting Lund's face it was written so close to her. "Any ward of the Council is deemed a ward for the remainder of their lives or until such time a coven can be found for them." She leaned back on her heels, her shawl drawn around her, face pinching in focus and determination. "This law is ancient, written over a thousand years ago, long prior to the founding of Coven Hall. Thus, this office must accept that law as writ."

"So mote it be," Gordon muttered.

"So mote it be," Gilleland and Carista said together.

"So," Lund snarled, eyes locked on me, "mote it be."

It sounded like she was choking on the words. I wished she'd succeed.

Not that it mattered. Vonda turned to me, Gordon joining her, and raised both hands. "Welcome, Ethpeal Hayle, daughter of all witches."

The Council power flared inside me.

She can never take this from you, Gordon said with grimness that almost hurt. Did she mean my mother or Lund? It didn't matter, not anymore. The Council Leader was right and no matter what, she'd given me the best chance anyone could have.

"Thank you," I said. *I won't let you down.*

Chapter Twenty-Four

Gordon cornered me on the way out, Gilleland and Carista remaining behind to talk with Lund after quietly congratulating me on this result. I was still in a bit of a daze, to be frank, so when Vonda hugged me tightly before pulling away, tears on her face, I didn't know what to say.

"What a Rhodes you would have made." She spun and fled then, the Council member weeping quietly as she exited, Gordon tucking her arm through mine and leading me away while I did my best to swallow my own grief.

"You're sure you're well?" Gordon let out a quick breath, shaking her head, smile wavering as her voice trembled just a little as she went on. "I honestly had no idea what would happen. I'm so sorry, Ethpeal, but it was last resort."

"The other territories turned me down?" That had to be the reason she risked it.

Her glum expression didn't last. "I should have just made you a ward in the first place," she said.

"But you didn't," I said, descending the stairs next to her, feeling her tense. "I take it there's a reason for that?" And here I thought my new optimism might stick? Instead, I found myself back in my old suspicious and cautious habits. Another thing to make Lund pay for at some point down the line. Oh, she would pay, even if I had to make her. "Let me guess, not everyone on Council agreed with the decision."

"I didn't give them a choice this time," she said. Then stopped and looked guilty.

"So, they rejected the idea originally." I nodded, hating the glum, dejected and numb feeling of expectations fulfilled. "I see."

"Ethpeal." Gordon turned me to confront her at the bottom of the steps, small face tight, power engulfing me, reminding me of what she'd done for me without having to say it, "this is a victory." I nodded. She was right, of course, and I had no right to be so downcast considering everything she'd done for me. I was still here and would remain here, thanks to her. "But I'm not going to mince words." I found myself tensing for the second shoe to hit the floor, with good reason. "Kirstin Lund will do everything in her power from this moment forward to convince the Council to break your guardianship and have you expelled permanently from Coven Hall. Without the ability to join another coven thanks to your mother," her tone told me what she thought of Mahalia, as did the fire suddenly burning in her eyes, "you will be on your own. And there will be nothing I or anyone else can do about it." I didn't say anything, so she carried on, accepting, I suppose, that I was listening and understood. Which I did, absolutely. "Focus on your studies," she said, "and survive the next three years. And then she will never be able to touch you again. No one will."

Because I would be an Enforcer. Message received and hope renewed, despite myself.

As I emerged at Gordon's side to the steps outside Massachusetts Hall, Varity nearly flew up the stairs toward me. I let the Council Leader go with a silent thank you and accepted my friend's hug without compunction, though her fury as she released me had me rocking back on my heels.

"Your mother," she snarled, "has a lot to answer for."

"She does." I raised my chin. "I'm sorry, Varity. You and your aunt went to a great deal of trouble for me. As did your leader. I let you down."

"You did nothing of the sort." Varity took the place Gordon had vacated, linking arms and leading me away. "I was really looking forward to having you in the family." Her sadness finally showed.

"I'm still your family," I said, meaning every word.

Varity's lips trembled, tears in her eyes, but she nodded, laughing. "You promise?"

"We're Enforcers," I said with great fierceness rising inside me. "That's a bond that will never be broken."

Varity stopped me in my tracks and hugged me all over again. She didn't let me go until I pushed her away, and I only did that because of the sight of Violet who'd come to a halt nearby. From her expression, Varity's older sister and heir to her coven wasn't exactly overjoyed to see me, but at least there wasn't animosity in her expression, only pity. I wasn't sure I was happy about that emotion aimed in my direction, however, and shrugged off the wave of feeling sorry for myself her attitude raised.

"Violet," I said, nodding to Varity. "I think your

sister wants to talk to you about me. If you'll excuse me." I walked away, head high, aiming for the portal to the Stronghold. I needed a solid dose of Enforcer magic and the massive power of that place right now, almost as much as I needed air to breathe. But as I approached, the sight of Demetrius Strong hurrying off in the opposite direction had me following.

Not because I wanted to talk to him, but because Burdie acted before I could stop her, the trigger of tainted magic she'd tied herself to acting like a rubber tether that forced my feet to follow despite myself.

Now, I trusted Demetrius at this point. There was no way I couldn't, not with our sorcery so closely enmeshed the last two times we'd met, or with the Enforcer fire linking us tightly together. He'd welcomed my offer of power and that meant there was no way he could hide from me. Didn't it? Burdie didn't seem to agree and, with a sigh and the mystery to distract me, despite my previous need to go home to the Stronghold, I followed my new friend to the border of the Yard.

I hesitated to cross the wards as I reached the edge, anticipating some pushback from Lund despite my recent status upgrade. I wasn't about to poke that particular bear so quickly, not when I felt wrung out from the Council power now that I had time for my adrenaline to retreat.

Fortunately, when I reached out to find him, I realized he hadn't left the wards after all but was following a path around the back of the campus, passing the line of trees at the far end of the Yard proper. I went after him, determined to answer my questions once and for all, coming up short when I saw him pause at the corner of a squat, stone building and address a robed figure.

I closed the distance, certain I was about to encounter one of the mysterious people he'd allowed inside the Stronghold the night before, only to recognize the power of the witch he spoke to even as Lisa Noe-Bradford looked up and waved at me with a weary smile.

"Ethpeal," she said, almost exasperated but amused enough I knew I wasn't in real trouble with her, "you'd think you would have had your fill of controversy for the day."

I stopped between them, Demetrius shrugging to our teacher while I squared my shoulders and nodded to the Enforcer professor.

"I was worried about my friend." I would not apologize for that. I had so few friends in my lifetime that now that I had some? I realized there was nothing I wouldn't do to protect them.

Noe-Bradford seemed to accept that easily, gesturing for me to come closer, which I did. "David and Kate seemed to think your insight bore weight, though I dissuaded them. Apparently, you are not dissuadable." She then tsked softly. "Perhaps your abilities make you an excellent addition to this conversation despite my trepidation."

Demetrius immediately reacted, shaking his head, anxious expression doing nothing to stop her from waving off his attempt to stop her.

"Professor," he said, faint groan in his tone.

"There are only two of you here," she said then, sounding reasonable. What did that mean? Wait, did she mean two sorcerers? Were we the only ones? "It makes sense to at least include Ethpeal, if only to protect her." Demetrius relented as Noe-Bradford faced me, blue eyes sparking with Enforcer fire. "First, you need to stop stalking Demetrius. He's following my orders and you're drawing attention to him that could put him in danger."

I swallowed in guilt. "I'm sorry."

She brushed that off, too. "Had I known your sorcery would make you suspicious, I would have taken steps," she said. "For now, here's what you need to know." She nodded to Demetrius. "Your story to tell."

He sighed softly, shrugged, blue eyes meeting mine. "My mother was a witch," he said, "but my father was a sorcerer. That's where my power came from. He was a member of an organization that I thought died out around the time he did. But they reached out to me the day before I left to come to Coven Hall, asking me to honor my father's promise to them."

"Which is?" I didn't like the sound of it at all.

"They're looking for someone," he said, "a prisoner in the Stronghold where no prisoner exists." Why did a face suddenly flash in my mind? Only to be gone again so quickly I barely remembered it happening, all tied to the blossom of darkness that writhed a moment before settling. "And they want me to help them find her."

A prisoner? I had no idea the Enforcer headquarters hosted a prison, though it made sense now that I thought about it. "Who are they?" For some reason, having an identifier for this mysterious community of sorcerers felt very important. As did the woman's face I'd now seen and couldn't seem to hold onto, still without any idea who she might be.

"They call themselves The Brotherhood," Demetrius said.

Any chance I had to bring up my question about the mysterious woman was burned away the moment he spoke as my grandmum flared, Burdie shrieking her fury.

CHAPTER TWENTY-FIVE

Neither of them seemed to notice my reaction, Demetrius carrying on as I fought with my great-grandmother over her spike of rage.

"I immediately contacted Professor Noe-Bradford," he said. "I suggested I play double agent and see if I could uncover what they wanted."

"It took some convincing," she said. "But you managed it." She sighed softly as she turned to me, Burdie's simmering anger just barely under control, her recognition of the name of the group in question making me anxious. "You're far too clever and observant for your own good, Ethpeal."

"I've had to watch my own back my entire life." I said it without thinking, and free of emotion, both of them visibly surprised by my candor while I brushed off their matching empathy. "I never intended to put you in danger. The opposite."

Demetrius nodded with a little, wry grin. "I know that," he said, his sorcery reaching out to mine. "But I couldn't tell you anything, not without permission."

"Now you know," Noe-Bradford said. "And you can stay out of it from now on."

"I could be of help." Of course, I instantly offered assistance while she shook her head, Demetrius' face more hopeful than I expected considering he'd tried to keep me from this whole situation just a moment ago.

"You're already on thin ice with Lund," she said. I sagged a little, knowing she was right, though Burdie's prodding had grown in pressure again. She wasn't about to let this go easily. "I don't want to risk putting you in a position that might threaten your place here. You're far too valuable to us, Ethpeal."

That was a nice platitude. "The Brotherhood." I spoke those two words together while Burdie writhed inside me. "There's history there, with my family." I had no idea what kind, but it was increasingly obvious.

Both of them seemed surprised by that,

Demetrius recovering more quickly.

"Considering you're a sorcerer as well as a witch," he said, "I guess that makes sense."

"And makes this as much my responsibility as yours," I said. What was I doing? Noc-Bradford was right. I didn't dare risk Lund's wrath right now. I might be an official inductee into Coven Hall for the moment, but one misstep and I knew she'd be taking her displeasure to the limit. Considering Gordon already confessed some of the Council members weren't happy about my presence here, it was likely Lund would get her way given the right argument and circumstance. But when I tried to explain the same to Burdie, she refused to listen.

"Ethpeal has a point." Demetrius took a step closer to me, blue eyes fixed on the professor whose obvious trepidation showed on her lovely face. "And I could use someone watching my back." Why had he changed his mind?

"Who are they looking for?" I didn't give her the opportunity to shut him down just yet, my question hovering there in the middle of our circle a long moment. Demetrius didn't answer, leaving it to his superior—our superior, I reminded myself— to decide if she was going to respond.

Which she finally did, though her tone was

dark, grim. "We don't know," she admitted. Demetrius shook his head in confirmation. "Not even the Brotherhood seem to know for certain."

How did that make any sense? "I don't understand."

"Neither do we," Demetrius told me, earnest but clearly determined to find out. "That's why the professor agreed to let me guide them into the Stronghold. Whatever this is about, we need answers before we can take further steps."

"If they don't know who it is they seek," I said, still flustered by this whole conversation, "how do they know what to look for?" It made zero sense to me at all.

"That's the thing," Demetrius said, frown creasing his face, aging him a little, his adorableness look fading into something darker and almost ancient to my surprise. "There's no record of a prisoner of the kind they described to me. Which can only mean one thing."

Noe-Bradford seemed reluctant to continue but did when he paused and waited for her to carry on. Such respect surely deserved a reward? She seemed to agree and grudgingly carried on, tucking herself deep inside her velvet cloak as she did.

"There's only one specific circumstance in which this makes any sense," she said. Stopped and then shook her head, taking a step back from both of us while Burdie seethed in anger at the professor's sudden change of heart. "None of which matters," she said. "You are ordered, Ethpeal Hayle, to stand down and stay out of it. No exceptions." Her eyes met mine with blue fire in them. "Am I completely understood?"

I wanted to fight her, not because of Burdie, either. My worry about Demetrius had taken hold and, I admit, my curiosity was tied to that. Not to mention the fact I'd spent most of my life standing aside and allowing things that I knew were wrong to unfold without doing anything about it out of a need to simply survive long enough to act at a later date.

This was a later date, and I was done being a spectator.

It was Demetrius who spoke for me. "I'm sure Ethpeal understands," he said. Then waited for me to agree.

I nodded at last, though it hurt me to do so, with an ache that stiffened my neck and shoulders, the strength it took to acquiesce physical and mental. "I understand," I said. Held the rest of my words inside. *But if the situation arises, I will act, and my future be damned.*

Noe-Bradford seemed to accept my words,

nodding to both of us and striding away while Demetrius waited for her to go before turning to me. His hand found mine, tugging me closer to him, smile returning, open and warm and full of delight.

"You can help me," he said then, "without breaking your word."

Was that mischief in his eyes? I found myself grinning back, that fierceness returned, Burdie wriggling in agreement. "What can I do?"

He glanced over his shoulder toward the retreating figure of our professor before speaking. "Help me find out who it is the Brotherhood are after," he said.

"How?" If he and the head of the Enforcer training program had failed to do so—and I highly doubted she'd kept the truth from the Enforcer leader himself, either—then what could I do?

"You're a ward of the Council," Demetrius said. "Which means you have access to all the records, and no one can stop you from looking at them."

That felt like we were on the border of breaking my promise, though I immediately set out, Demetrius at my side keeping pace. "You think the person's identity will be there?"

"Not exactly," he said. "It will be the absence of their identity we're looking for."

He'd totally lost me. "I'm still confused."

Demetrius nodded as we entered the main Yard and headed for University Hall. "Here's the truth of it," he said, voice low as we passed a small knot of normal students chatting under a tree. I couldn't imagine a life where my only concern was what classes to take and if the boy that I liked felt the same in return. Yes, I had those pressures, and so much more. "The only way that this is possible is if the Council removed all memory of the person in question from the records and from the minds of every magical soul involved."

Wait, was that even possible? "Why would they do such a thing?" The thought was utterly inconceivable to me. How would one even go about the task? Burdie snarled at me to pay attention and not get distracted.

"There was a time," Demetrius said, "when that was the punishment for the worst criminals. Complete and utter eradication from history."

That was… horrific. And made me think of my mother. What would my life be like without memories of Mahalia Hayle in my mind? I shuddered from the thought despite the fact its appeal almost outweighed its diabolical truth. "To wipe someone from existence so completely." Bile rose in my throat, made me swallow twice, while

Demetrius paused, pulling me to a stop before we reached the steps to the hall in question.

"I know." He gave me a moment to collect myself. "That's why it's not done anymore. The rule was added to the Council laws twenty years ago."

It took a few calming breaths for his words to penetrate, but when they did, I understood his meaning immediately. "Twenty years ago," I said. "You think whoever it is the Brotherhood is seeking was the reason the law was changed at that time."

He nodded with some enthusiasm, smile returning despite the subject matter. "I'm hoping what's missing from the records might give us clues as to who it was they removed and why the law was changed."

It was a long shot. Finding something visible wasn't always easy. Uncovering something eradicated and erased on purpose? Worse than a hunt for a needle in a haystack. And yet, I found myself infected by his excitement at the prospect of discovery and nodded in response.

"Let's see what we can uncover," I said, turning to climb the steps.

He caught my arm, tugged me back, serious and focused, voice very soft and clearly only for my ears.

I shivered as his sorcery tied into mine, the scent of berries and mint and something sweet passing between us.

"I'm putting you at risk asking," he said. "No matter what, if we start digging, there's a chance we uncover something Lund could use against you." Guilt passed over his face and he hesitated while I scowled back.

"And she could find anything at any moment to that end," I said. "I won't stand by and let her make me a coward. Or let her interfere with living my life as I see fit." This opportunity to take action, even if it wasn't direct, wasn't something I was willing to retreat from. Maybe it was recklessness fed by frustration or my desire to show Lund she couldn't bully me like my mother had. Perhaps it was friendship, loyalty, or Burdie's persistent influence. Whatever the case, I was done standing aside and biding my time. "Are you coming or not?"

He flashed me a grin and nodded, following me up the steps while I marched toward the task like it might mean my doom.

Chapter Twenty-Six

I suppose I should have been trepidatious about entering the archive, but when the Council's power welcomed me with open arms, any nervousness about Demetrius' request fell to the wayside. The archivist ignored us both, nodding at us as we passed, the elderly witch only holding one finger to her lips as the door slid shut behind us, dull thud of its closing making more noise than she was willing to allow.

With that initial hurdle over and my confidence growing past the determined stubbornness that carried me this far, Demetrius and I quickly located the stacks we needed, the categorization of historical data incredibly easy to navigate. He showed me how to trigger timelines with magic and all we had to do was follow the trail of blue sparks through the tall, parallel bookshelves to the section in question, the glowing dates on the markers lighting up with the exact timing we needed.

Here's the law's enactment, Demetrius said, unrolling a scroll and showing me the details.

How did you know about this? I took the roll from him and read through the excessively flowery language, confirming what he'd already told me, the droning voice of an elderly witch in the back of my mind intoning the prose as the magic embedded in it unfolded history for me.

I stumbled on it in an old text in the library, he sent back, taking down another scroll and perusing it with a skim of power before replacing it with a little frown, selecting a heavy leather tome instead. *Mention of the change in law, but that was it. I haven't been able to get permission to check out this archive until now.*

Not even Noe-Bradford could get you in? That seemed odd.

I haven't told her about it, he confessed, blue eyes wide with guilt. *I wanted to find evidence first before I did. I've already asked her to take a great risk letting me front this whole process. She and Leader Donovan agreed, but only because she supported me to the Enforcer leader. If I can come up with answers, maybe it will help wrap this up before they have to step in. It sounded like he really wanted that outcome.*

You feel responsible, I sent, setting aside the original scroll and taking down a book of my own. Power zinged across my palms as I opened it, another witch's voice, this one higher pitched, telling me about coven updates and Council business that almost numbed my brain in its dullness.

My father was Brotherhood, Demetrius sent with a hint of steel in his mental voice, my sorcery sliding over his in sympathetic response. *Whoever this person is they seek, I can only imagine they earned their punishment.*

The Brotherhood. I shivered as Burdie snarled something I didn't catch. *Seems a stupid way to punish someone*, I sent offhand. *Wiping them from memory. How can we learn from the past if we're not allowed to remember it?* Exactly why the idea of losing my memories of my mother might appeal on a certain level but bring me a horror I couldn't comprehend on another. Imagine if I forgot how cruel and evil she truly was? And why I was so intent on being the best witch, the best Enforcer, I could be?

I'd lose a part of me I'd never recover and couldn't bear to part with, frankly. No matter my mother's evil and mania, I deserved the right to deal with those memories as I saw fit and use them to strengthen me, if that was my choice. Having that option stripped from me seemed the basest kind of disenfranchisement I could imagine.

Demetrius seemed to agree. *That's why the law was changed*, he sent. *Apparently, the Council of the day thought the same way we do. Though too late, it seems, for our purposes.*

How is it these Brotherhood members know about this person, then? Burdie had become more accustomed to the use of the word and didn't give me the hard time she had been all along, listening intently instead.

I don't know the exact mechanics of it, Demetrius admitted, taking down another book while I replaced the one I'd perused at the specific date— September, actually, the fourth of the month, a match to the day of this very one I lived if twenty years in the past. *All I do know is for whatever reason, by design, I have to believe, several Brotherhood members were made aware of the prisoner's existence three days ago and that triggered this entire venture.*

Three days ago, I sent. *You're aware we're on the very day of the law's enactment?*

He nodded to me, grim again. *I am*, he sent. *That's part of the reason I'm so intent on this, Ethpeal. I have no proof, of course, but it's far too coincidental, don't you think? I have this terrible feeling something is about to happen and if I can't come up with answers...* he trailed off, sighing softly into the still and dull air of the archive, hands sliding over another book before he bypassed it and carried on. *I feel responsible, yes. You're right. My father was Brotherhood, and not a good person. I've spent my life trying to live up to my mother's name and her kindness despite him.* His blue eyes glowed as they turned to me. *I know you know how I feel.*

There was no need to respond to that whatsoever, because he was absolutely right. *And the Brotherhood themselves? Who are they?*

He flipped through some pages, sparks climbing over the yellowed sheets. *A collective of sorcerers,* he sent, *ancient, as our Councils are ancient. Sorcery isn't bad, inherently.* Burdie snorted at that. *But its action requires the destruction of elements in order to work. Metal, stone, plants, etc.* So, that much of my very thin education had been correct. *Every sorcerer has their own specialty.* He winked at me. *If you're nice, I'll help you figure out yours, if you want.*

Burdie grumbled but didn't argue. *And yours is?*

I'm an all-elements sorcerer, he sent then, softly

and without pride. *Like my father.* He hesitated before the blossom of his power prodded mine. *I think you might be, too.*

Is he right? I aimed that question at my great-grandmother who didn't respond. That was answer enough. *What does that mean?* That was for Demetrius.

We'll talk about it more when this is over, he sent. *It's important for you to know, Ethpeal. To have control of all your magicks. Sorcery is stronger, in a way, than witch power, but very different and it's often dormant in witches unless something traumatic occurs.*

Like losing one's family, I sent.

Or having one's family's power stripped to benefit another. There was enough of a rage undercurrent in him I found myself reaching out to touch his hand. He recovered quickly, but couldn't hide it from me, not completely, our magic tied so closely together now I could feel the beating of his heart. *That's neither here nor there,* he sent. *Our circumstances aside, it means that we are in a unique position to master multiple magicks. I choose to see that as a good thing.*

I couldn't help but agree with him. And almost said so, only to hear Demetrius gasp audibly, the first sound either of us had made out loud, catching my attention as he spun with a tight grin, a scroll in his hands.

Listen to this, he sent, tugging my fingers toward the parchment. The moment I connected, the same elderly witch's voice began its drone.

And so, it was decided, she recorded, *that so forth would the act of erasure be eliminated from the laws of the Council and that revision would hence be named the* Attica Brindle Amendment *as the only reminder permitted of the final soul to endure such a fate.*

Attica Brindle, Demetrius sent. While a chill climbed my spine, the woman's face flashing in my mind all over again.

Brindle, Burdie whispered, fury unrepentant.

GrandMum, I sent to her. *We have to talk.*

Chapter Twenty-Seven

As much as we dug, there wasn't anything else to find. Demetrius admitted defeat when his stomach began to grumble, though I stubbornly clung to the idea we might find more with a bit of time.

She's gone, Ethpeal, he sent, shaking his head, blond curls dull in the low light of the archive's quiet chamber. *But we have a name now.* He seemed buoyed by that fact. *I might be able to use it somehow when I return to the Stronghold. There's so much power in a name, even one that's been erased so thoroughly from the rest of history.*

The fact they'd left that single reference to the woman in question led me to believe there were more threads in that magic to be pulled. Not to mention the fact I was now certain whoever the strange woman was I seemed to be tied to in some way was, if not the woman we sought, at least connected to her. Why then did my thoughts about her seem to elude me and the opportunities to mention her to Demetrius come and go without me saying a word? I had to believe it was tied to the spell the Council had cast. There may even have been a way to reverse it, who knew? I followed him with reluctance as he departed the archive, returning to the Yard and heading for Annenberg Hall and the task of satisfying our bellies while my mind remained divided.

Burdie's choice to ignore me when I again prodded her to talk wasn't lost on me, and when I'd suggested we share what she knew with Demetrius she'd fallen silent again, almost eerily so. That meant she didn't trust him, didn't it? The echo of who my great-grandmother had been didn't carry all the depths of her personality, only the more ego-bearing judgments and protection-focused ideologies, so it was understandable why she'd want to keep him out of our conversation. Still, this was his task, and he'd proven himself trustworthy, as far as I was concerned, so she had to know whatever she told me I'd be sharing with him regardless.

Why not just cut out the middlewitch and take care of it all at once?

She continued to refuse, and I wasn't about to abandon him just yet, so our talk would have to wait. It was Thaddea who suggested my stubbornness came naturally to me and we were both being ridiculous, but Burdie started it.

Contrary ancestress.

Varity and Deloras joined us as we sat to eat our early supper, neither of us bringing up the circumstance we'd found ourselves in, Jeffery seating himself between Demetrius and me, though without any kind of animosity behind his choice, I was certain. I wasn't until we'd finished devouring our meals and I stood abruptly to go, catching my co-conspirator's eye, that Varity spoke up.

"You two have been thick as thieves since we sat down," she said. "What's going on?"

Had I hidden my impatience and subtle attempts to keep silent so poorly then? My mask had failed me, the one I'd nurtured for so long. Then again, perhaps it had never done the job I hoped, and I hadn't been fooling anyone despite my best efforts in that regard. Whatever the case, if I was slipping, so be it, though I wished I'd managed a bit better, just for a short time longer.

Deloras seemed surprised by Varity's demand,

though Jeffery wasn't shocked in the least, nodding in agreement.

"You're up to something," he said, looking back and forth between me and Demetrius, before glaring in my direction. "Tell me you're still not on about Dee being some kind of problem."

"Not at all," I said. "It was a misunderstanding." I stood there, almost sat again, knowing my awkwardness wasn't helping my case any. "We're just in the middle of some research."

"For the professor." Demetrius swept to his feet, smiling at our friends, nodding. "A pre-class project, is all."

Jeffery's frown didn't fade, Varity's face screwing up in a doubtful scowl, but I didn't give either of them a chance to challenge us further.

"We really need to finish before she asks why we're late." I hurried off, hoping Demetrius would follow, his steady presence at my side by the time we exited into the yard. He chuckled a little, low and lovely, the sound sending shivers up my spine. Our power twined more tightly together as he walked close beside me, this odd camaraderie so delicious I never wanted it to end.

"You're really terrible at subterfuge," he said.

"So it seems." I stopped outside the chapel and inhaled. "There's something I need to tell you and I don't want you to freak out at me."

He shrugged. "I've told you a few things that deserve the same treatment," he said. "Go ahead."

"I can talk to the Stronghold." I waited for him to say something, only to have Demetrius stand quietly and without judgment while I drew another shaking breath and went on. "I plan to ask it where she is."

That made his eyes fly wide and a huge grin burst over his face. "Brilliant!"

I smiled tentatively back. "You don't think me mad."

"I don't." He gestured, blue fire opening the portal to the very place I planned to go next. "I'm sorry you doubt me still."

I grasped his arm before he could pass through, making him wait, heart beating a little fast before I hugged him. I rarely did so of my own volition, and that made the gesture feel unnatural. Except, the moment my arms closed around him, our power's connection made embracing Demetrius the most normal and natural thing in the world.

He hugged me back with gentle pressure and full commitment before releasing me. "Thank you," he said.

Did he know how much trust it took for me to show that level of vulnerability? Of course, he did.

My power told him so.

I waved toward the portal and managed another small smile, my heartrate still giving me some trouble for a variety of reasons I wasn't willing to explore just yet. "After you," I said.

"No, please," he laughed with a sweeping bow toward me, "after *you.*"

I was giggling when I crossed through.

Welcome home, the Stronghold sent. My laughter died immediately, though not from its tone, but from the weight of contact. So much pressure despite its gentle touch.

I need your help, I sent, sharing the encounter with Demetrius through our combined power as I hurried toward my quarters, head down and avoiding the other Enforcers we encountered going about their own business. The stone halls of the Stronghold seemingly teemed with activity suddenly, despite its size and it took several moments before we found somewhere we could be alone.

Meanwhile, the fortress' answer had me excited all over again. *Of course*, it sent. *What do you need of me?*

We're seeking someone, I sent. *A prisoner. Her name is Attica Brindle.*

The Stronghold didn't answer for a long

moment. *Your granddaughter's soul is a match to yours in many ways*, it sent.

My...? *What does that mean?*

Your descendants have run these halls, do so even now, it went on, as though my confusion meant nothing to it. *So much darkness is coming, but you are the Light before she can be. Until she comes to me. She is here now, as are you, though the day is not yet of the coming of the Light.* It sighed deeply, a long and achingly sorrowful sound. *You do not comprehend. Time is linear to you. No matter.* I spluttered in response, terror winding its fingers through me despite my confusion. For some reason, mention of Dark and Light triggered a visceral reaction inside me that had me dreading the future as much as wondering what was to come for me.

Do you know of whom we seek? Demetrius seemed as freaked out by the conversation as I was, though at least he managed to stay on track.

The Stronghold's response didn't arrive before the touch of Noe-Bradford's mind interrupted.

I need to see you, she sent to my friend and companion.

On my way, professor. He met my eyes with his blue ones, frustration there. "Don't do anything without me."

I nodded and let him go, watching him hurry

off, while the Stronghold remained silent. When he was finally gone, though not completely, the hum of his magic still tied to me, I returned my attention inward.

What else can you tell me? I meant about Attica Brindle. Didn't I?

Only that you are beloved, the Stronghold sent, *as she is, and she is more than worthy of you and the faith they place in her. She bears the weight as though born to it. Because she is.*

Who? It might have been making me uncomfortable, but I was now incredibly curious. *My granddaughter?* Who, I wondered, would be her grandfather? A silly aside that wasn't worthy of me.

You will fear for her, it sent. *But she will save us all.* It paused then. *Or not. The future is not yet decided. Still, I choose to believe. As I believe your friend is in need of you.* I blinked at the shift in conversation. *More than you know, now and evermore, but now, most especially.*

Demetrius is in trouble? I spun and went after him, banishing thoughts of what might be, of Attica and the mystery of the Brotherhood, even as I felt shock ripple through our combined power, Demetrius' surprise and a blaze of anger that was silenced before I could find out the cause. I stumbled at the severance of our magics, cursing softly and hurrying even more, coming into the meeting room at the exact moment Ivan Dumont pointed a finger at Demetrius with his big voice booming.

"We have a traitor among us," he said, "and I demand the Enforcer order do something about it."

Chapter Twenty-Eight

What was Ivan thinking? I stormed toward him, Demetrius quiet under the sudden scrutiny, even as Noe-Bradford stepped in before I could reach my friend and lose my mind on the Dumont witch challenging him.

My, how the tables had turned.

"Evidence, Mr. Dumont." She gestured to the tall Enforcer trainee. "In my office."

He seemed to hesitate before speaking again. "He's been associating with sorcerers," Ivan said, not a trace of apology in his voice.

Where did he get his information? Panic almost choked me while I skidded to a halt at Demetrius' side. Ivan glanced my way but didn't seem surprised to find me there.

"I said my office," our professor growled at him.

Ivan finally nodded and followed her, Demetrius going along without being asked. I caught Jeffery's arm and shook my head, but he brushed me off.

"Dee might trust you," he said, "but that doesn't mean you get to tell me what to do, Ethpeal." Jeffery stalked off after the trio, though I was fairly certain Noe-Bradford would complete the denial I'd tried to spare him. No way was she going to allow him to hear a word of what Ivan had to say.

Which meant I wouldn't be privy either.

I can tell you what she says. The Stronghold's deep voice cracked like old granite grinding against itself.

Of course, it could. *Let me listen.* I hurried off, ignoring everyone around me, Varity nowhere in sight, fortunately. Not that I didn't want her around, but too worried about Demetrius to think of anyone else at the moment. By the time I reached my quarters and closed the door behind me, Noe-Bradford's voice was speaking in my mind and an image of her standing beside a desk, the two Enforcer trainees lined up in front of her, flashed in my head.

"Explain yourself, Mr. Dumont." Our professor

had crossed her arms over her chest, her tone low and unhappy. "Accusing another student of wrongdoing publicly, without proof provided to your instructor, goes against every tenant of Enforcer code."

"I'm sorry, professor," Ivan said, sounding not the least bit contrite. I fumbled my way to my bed and sat down, the odd juxtaposition of the view in my mind and my reality making walking difficult. I managed it as Ivan went on. "I have it on good authority Demetrius Strong has been aiding and abetting a troublesome group of sorcerers known as the Brotherhood."

"I see," Noe-Bradford said. "According to whom?"

"I can't reveal my source," Ivan said. I wasn't the only one who found that reply arrogant.

"You will explain yourself," the professor snarled, "or you will discover which of the pair of you will end up out of this order, young man. Answer me."

Ivan hesitated before speaking, but he did answer. "My cousin, Odette, is student assistant to Headmistress Lund," he said. "According to records, Demetrius' father, Able Strong, was a member of that order."

"And?" Noe-Bradford's power practically

crackled with irritation. I was very grateful she was on our side. What was Ivan thinking? Clearly, Odette had been stirring trouble. But why? What did she hope to gain from this?

Ivan seemed surprised by the professor's reaction. "You knew?"

"I know everything about my students," she shot back. "Including the fact your family is in the process of absorbing what remains of Mr. Strong's. Correct?" Ivan nodded slowly, face creasing in a frown. "And since your cousin is heir to the Dumont family, she has a vested interest in those about to be included in your coven. Yes?" Again, he nodded, though his frown had taken a darker turn. Aimed at who, I wondered? Odette might be in for a very bad time of things. At least, that was my impression as Noe-Bradford went on. "All of this smacks of family politics," she said, "and considering your plan is to become an Enforcer, Mr. Dumont, untethered to that family, I would hope you would choose your order over the coven you've decided to forsake for this role."

"I'm sorry, professor," Ivan said, somewhat contrite. "You're right, of course. However—"

"However, nothing," she silenced him instantly, shutting him down with a sharp chop of one hand. "So, Mr. Strong's father was Brotherhood. Do you know what that means?"

Ivan shook his head.

"I see," she said. "All you know is his deceased parent was a member of an order of sorcerers who you have no further information about."

Ivan's face had turned very red. "I was told they were problematic."

"You are very trusting," she said, though the word *gullible* wasn't spoken and perhaps should have been, "and easily manipulated by someone who has an ulterior motive. Should I be further concerned about you, Mr. Dumont? Do you have the wellbeing of this order and your fellow trainees at heart? Or do you have a continuing conflict of interest I must address for the welfare of your classmates?"

Ivan seemed to finally take her threat seriously, turning immediately to Demetrius. "My deepest apologies," he said, addressing the smaller trainee for the first time. "I was led to believe your attachment to that organization might be detrimental to our order."

"Were I of the Brotherhood," Demetrius said, "your information might be correct. They are problematic, though I am not and never have been a member of that group. My father's decisions are not mine, Ivan. No more than yours are your family's. I would hope."

Ivan appeared shaken by the whole thing, bowing to the professor with a grim expression. "I've shamed myself in this matter," he said. "You're correct, ma'am. Please accept my apology and be assured it will never happen again."

Noe-Bradford softened a little, though her expression remained tight and grim. "Let this be a lesson to you, Mr. Dumont. And you, Mr. Strong. The Enforcer family deserves your commitment and your confidence. You two have been at odds since you joined us last year and I'm tired of it." They had? Perhaps that was the reason Odette decided to try to make trouble for Demetrius. It was obvious to me she had uncomfortable feelings for her cousin. Could this have been some kind of power move to elevate Ivan? "I would think you'd both be well aware that kind of behavior is intolerable in second year students." Neither of them moved a muscle. "When you both take on the full mantle of your positions, you must be able to trust one another and rely on each other for support and protection. This kind of petty squabbling can get you killed in the field. Do you understand?"

"Yes, professor," they said together.

She sighed, rubbing at her eyes with her thumb and forefinger. "This is no coven you've signed up for, no collective with a leader too weak to moderate its members. This is the Enforcer order, and it is that power that chooses who is worthy. If you doubt even for a moment that magic's ability to discern those deserving of its fire, it's time to turn around and walk through the door and go back to the covens that bore you."

Ivan and Demetrius both nodded, Ivan turning and striding out, though my friend lingered.

"That could have gone badly," he said.

Noe-Bradford seemed anxious in response. "I don't want you to meet the Brotherhood tonight," she said. "Whatever the Dumonts were after sending Ivan after you like that, make no mistake, it was on purpose."

"Odette is just being Odette," Demetrius said. "She was born to manipulate others while stirring the pot."

The professor nodded her agreement, though she didn't seem to have changed her mind on the matter. "Be careful," she said. "If Odette Dumont *is* watching, this could all blow up before we find out what the Brotherhood is actually after."

I was surprised when Demetrius didn't tell her what we'd discovered, my friend simply shrugging.

"If they ask me to meet," he said, "I can't turn them down."

She huffed a breath then tossed her hands. "Very well. Keep me in the loop, Demetrius. I don't want you to be solo on this. Whatever happens, this was my decision to allow you to carry on and I won't see you bear the brunt of blame if something goes wrong."

"Thank you, professor." He exited, the vision fading as the Stronghold released me from the images. I blinked into the room's soft light, disoriented suddenly from being back in this space, alone and in total quiet.

Demetrius. I reached out to him, only to have him cut me off, gently but with purpose.

Time for you to do as the professor commanded, he sent. *I have a name, now, Ethpeal, because of you. Thank you for that. But I won't involve you further.* Was he thinking about the Dumonts? He had to be.

I'm not afraid of Odette Dumont. I'd faced far worse at home.

Nor am I, he sent, sounding unsurprised I'd made that leap. Did he know I'd been eavesdropping? *But you were born to be an Enforcer and if you disobey Noe-Bradford, there's a chance you won't get to find out what that could mean.*

I doubted she'd kick me out for helping him regardless of what she'd said but had to retreat when he finally cut me off completely and left me, scowling at the floor and with pent-up anger needing release. And I knew exactly who I could take it out on.

Except when I went hunting for Ivan, I couldn't find him. The coward was clearly hiding somewhere. Very well, probably for the best he put himself out of my reach until I cooled off. I spent the rest of the evening with Varity and Deloras at the cafe, listening to them chatter while my mind spun, worry for Demetrius giving me a headache and finally sending me to bed early.

I fell asleep almost immediately, though I woke with a start quite suddenly to the soft sound of Varity snoring in the bed across from me, the darkened sky outside not quite the same black as what I was used to on my own plane. My Fey blood allowed for some vision in the dimness, enough when I sat up, surprised to find myself wide awake, I had no trouble seeing the room around me.

I half-expected to find someone there, shivering, though it only took a moment for me to realize the person I anticipated wasn't in my room directly.

It *was* my room.

You asked me earlier about Attica Brindle, the

Stronghold sent.

I did. I pushed the blankets away, staring up at the ceiling as though that might direct my attention more clearly toward its massive presence.

Odd, it took me some time to uncover her. It seemed perplexed by the conundrum. *I have no barriers to time and space, however that soul I lost for a time. How remarkable.*

The witch Council erased her from history, I sent.

That shouldn't affect me, the Stronghold told me without arrogance. *However, it would appear it has. Until now. I have found the one you seek, in my tower. Would you like to meet her?*

I leaped to my feet, body tingling all over. *Are you kidding me?*

I didn't mean to jest. Its tone was almost pained.

Sorry, I sent, pulling on my clothing, slipping out of the room as quietly as possible so as not to wake Varity. *Can you reach Demetrius?*

He is outside the plane at the moment, the Stronghold sent. *Would you like to wait for him?*

No, I sent, feet already carrying me forward though I didn't know where I was going. I debated briefly bringing Noe-Bradford in on the hunt, only to shake that off. I'd find the location and then fetch Demetrius and together we'd deliver the trouble the Brotherhood stirred to the Enforcer order. From the sound of his history, like me, he'd been powerless despite himself for a long time. He deserved to be the hero for once. *Take me there now, please.*

As you wish. I realized I was walking in the right direction when it applied some pressure to my mind, Burdie and Thaddea both reacting with eagerness, so I wasn't as concerned as I probably should have been. It wasn't every night a gargantuan power that embodied a vast fortress on a foreign plane of existence outside time and space chose to be your guide on a quest of any kind. Was it wrong I felt a giddy excitement rise within me? Yes, I was breaking the command Noe-Bradford laid out for me, but then again, *was* I? Sophistry in hand, it could be argued that I wasn't doing anything of the sort. Demetrius and his Brotherhood contacts were nowhere to be found. I was merely going to the source of their search.

I was very good, it seemed, at making excuses for bad behavior.

Chapter Twenty-Nine

Whether the Stronghold itself chose to lead me down a path that didn't include other Enforcers or I simply lucked out, whatever the case, I found myself passing through a narrow doorway into a circular chamber without encountering another soul. As I looked up the long, winding staircase that climbed into dimness above me, I felt another shiver, this one of nervousness, though it didn't stop me from pursuing the inevitable.

To the top, the Stronghold sent.

I paced my way upward, doing my best not to rush, already feeling the burn in my legs after only a pair of stories. It seemed to ascend forever, the climb almost meditative after a while, the ache in my thighs matching the measured inhales and exhales of my lungs as I circled my way to the top.

When I finally found myself on a landing, after passing multiple doorways the Stronghold encouraged me to ignore, I had to take a moment to get my bearings, the rounded way of walking making me a bit unsteady on my now tingling feet. When I finally pushed through the last door at the top of the steps, I felt a rush of magic engulf me when I did, not Enforcer by any means. No, this was the power of the Stronghold itself, and when I walked through to the other side I had the distinct impression I'd not just entered a room, but yet another plane all together.

Very good, Ethpeal, it sent. *Fourth cell on the left. She's waiting for you.* It sounded suddenly curious.

She knew I was coming? How?

Apparently, the Stronghold sent. *I have no explanation.*

"Come," a voice said, a woman's voice, echoing from down the corridor. I stepped forward without realizing I'd done so, approaching slowly, heart racing for other reasons than the climb I'd just endured. "I feel you, daughter. Come to me, Ethpeal."

Wait, she knew my name? I stopped at the barred door the Stronghold indicated, finding it harder to breathe now than it had been all those steps below.

"Attica," I whispered.

"Indeed." She came into view, dark hair in ribbons of curls around her face, black eyes shining from the other side of the bars. I reached out and touched the door, fingers burning with blue fire and sparks as I did and I shuddered back from contact, my Enforcer magic suddenly alive and furious. "I should have warned you." She laughed, a deep and throaty sound, that had me hitching my breath. "Welcome, Ethpeal. To my personal hell." She gestured at the door. "I'd share power, my dear, but as you can see…"

Open it, I sent to the Stronghold.

I don't think that's a good idea, it answered.

Wait, it was right. What was I thinking? "How did you know I was coming?"

Attica simply shrugged. "I felt your power when you touched my token." Her what? "Your power was simply too strong for me to ignore. I've visited your dreams, as well." She had. I shook my head, feeling disoriented, one hand rising to press to my skull. Something was wrong with me, a dullness seeping at me, drawing out my soul. Even Burdie and Thaddea were quiet, so quiet. "And you impressed me, my dear, when you entered the

Stronghold the first time." She almost sounded hungry. "The strength of it reverberated through the very rocks of this place." My induction into the Enforcer order. Had it such far-reaching repercussions? "I recognized your magic immediately, of course. You have much of your great-grandmother in you, my dear. Tell me, how is Auburdeen?"

"Dead," I managed, barely. What was wrong with me?

She sighed a little as the echo inside me writhed at my answer. "A pity," she said. "She and I never had the chance to meet, though she knew my father very well." She leaned close to the bars but made no attempt to touch them. "I would have told her of Samuel Brindle's ultimate fate and her part in it if I'd been given the chance."

That sounded ominous enough, and even Burdie quailed, rousing a moment to do so before sighing and sinking deep inside me once again. "I don't know who that is." My voice sounded thin in my ears, muffled.

"Witches and their secrets." Attica snorted softly, tossed her head, curls bouncing as she retreated. I watched her sit on a low bench, the room on the other side of the bars spare and sparse, though livable. A food tray sat on the table next to her, so someone was feeding her, caring for her. But who? "When I was leader of the Brotherhood, I had no such insistence on keeping things so quiet."

"Is that part of the reason you're here?" That dazed feeling increased, and no matter what I did, I couldn't seem to shake it, as though a veil had fallen over my mind, a mist rising to consume my resistance. I needed to step back, take a moment, ward myself. Clearly, she was a force to be reckoned with whether locked up or not. Instead, I took a half of a shuffling step closer, careful not to touch the bars this time, swaying as the dullness increased. "Why did they remove you from history?" My lips felt numb, the words tumbling out through lips that felt almost too thick to work.

She sat back, crossing one leg over the other, black coverall fitted to her tall, lean shape. "None of that matters," she said, watching me carefully.

"It does to me." I fought for it to, however. What was wrong with me? Burdie now utterly silent, Thaddea the only echo inside me to show any liveliness and even she barely struggled against this lethargy that overcame us more by the moment. Even the Stronghold's presence had faded from me while Attica Bridle seemed to consume my attention completely.

"Very well," she said. "No one remembers my legacy, thanks to the Council and their lack of foresight. Perhaps it makes sense to finally be remembered, especially by one with whom I have such a long family tie." I still didn't know what that meant. What had her father and my grandmum to do with one another? I'd only known of sorcery because of stories I'd heard from Sassafras, really, and rumors in the coven about Burdie's magic. What was missing from those stories?

"You remember," I said.

"I do," she snarled back at me, "they made sure of that. The real punishment, they said." She cackled a laugh that ended in a scowl devoid of humor. "That I would always remember, always be here, trapped in limbo, in time forgotten, fed and clothed and cared for by magic forever, until the very Stronghold itself collapsed when the Universe did, forgotten by all except, of course, myself."

"That's despicable," I said, barely managing it, feeling tears prickle my eyes in sympathy. I meant it. What had they done to her? How dared they?

"It is," Attica agreed with me, tone now light and almost amused. Her mood had shifted so quickly I had an insight I wasn't expecting despite my addled mind. She'd been alone here for twenty years. Had she lost her mind in that time? The possibility was excellent, though if she was already mad when she came in... "Thank you for that, Ethpeal. Not everyone would have such empathy." She shrugged. "If they could remember me, that is. But not even the witches who trapped me here recall their reasons. The fools."

I had to agree with her again. "Are you going to tell me why they did this to you?" It felt very important she answer that question. And then, suddenly.

It didn't. Nothing mattered, not really. I felt my knees wobble, all the strength nearly gone from my thighs, and I wavered in place, feeling darkness encroaching on me, on the verge of passing out.

"In due time," she said. "I'm rather enjoying your company. After all, it took me long enough to lure you here, my dear."

Lure me? I shook my head at her, that motion snapping me briefly back into focus, though it didn't last. "What do you mean?"

"I'm the reason you're an Enforcer, silly," she said in a breathy tone, wriggling her fingers at me. "You're here because I wanted you to be here. You're welcome."

Any other response might have meant my end. If she'd only chosen another attitude, her own form of compassion, she likely would have succeeded in her plan to subdue me. But she chose to be like Mahalia and, in doing so, reversed her control over me in a pounding heartbeat that had me gasping and shuffling back from the door. As soon as I did, I felt a measure better and threw my rejection at her, insides writhing against this odd hold she had over me.

"That's not true." My entire being shrieked in denial, against the control she suggested, the power over me she claimed. "I'm here because I wanted to come here." To Coven Hall, to be an Enforcer. To the Stronghold. To her cell.

Her lips twisted bitterly before Attica laughed in a sudden shrill way that had my teeth grating against one another as I slid back another step, feeling myself wake further. "Oh, do lighten up, won't you? At least I know you're not gullible. Not like your great-grandmother was."

What game was she playing? Of course, she hadn't influenced me. She was toying with me, seeing what she could get away with. I shook off the rest of the fuzzy feeling, taking a final solid step away from her door, and heard her snarl in response. The moment I did, my mind cleared the rest of the way and only then did I realize the truth.

"You figured out how to seep sorcery out under the wards of your cell." I could see it now that I knew it was there, the filthy film of it staining the stones before her door, writhing and undulating in encouragement, luring me to come forward and stand in its presence once more.

"Clever, clever Ethpeal." Attica didn't sound like she meant that kindly. "Your mind, your power, are exactly what I need to make the Brotherhood great again."

I clenched myself against the emotions wanting to emerge in response, to scream in Burdie's voice as my great-grandmother returned to her own presence and rejected Attica's words utterly. There was a story here I didn't know, one that I needed to know. I had wanted to talk to my grandmum and I'd failed to force that conversation. The echo must have forgotten as well, hardly surprising since the majority of who she had been was already gone. Echoes tended to react in the moment, rarely commanded any kind of presence of mind, so I could hardly blame her for failing to fill me in before now.

This situation was on me wholly and completely.

"You made me forget you," I said.

Attica snorted. "It wasn't hard," she said. "The Council's stupid spell made it simple, in fact. A bit of encouragement was all it took to keep you from being too curious when I needed you to let it go. But all that's changed now, Ethpeal."

"Tell me the truth," I said, sensing no concern from the Stronghold despite the sorcery puddling outside Attica's cell. Surely it would sense if there was any danger past the small space she'd managed, in twenty years, to invade? I had to trust it, even if I couldn't trust her. "Why did they imprison you and leave you here this way?"

Attica stood and crossed to the door. I kept a careful eye on the border of her reaching sorcery, but the tentacles didn't respond to her proximity, so obviously it was the ward at the bars themselves that held her power where it was. Not that I felt any less threatened by her presence there. Was it Burdie's warning inside me that had me rubbing at goosebumps on my arms as Attica's black eyes fixed me with burning hate?

"I simply attempted to incorporate sorcery with witchcraft, like dear old daddy tried to do." She shrugged. "He failed, but I found a way to succeed."

"How?" There had to be more to it. There was no way the Council would act with such swift and horrible action if she'd merely been dabbling in magic bonding. Surely, doing so was a good thing? How many witches would live fuller magical lives if they had access to powers lying dormant inside? I know I appreciated very much the three magicks that I now had full access to.

"Witches fear change like nothing else," she hissed at me, though I had a feeling it wasn't me she meant that poisonous tone for. "Any attempt to improve the lot of those not inside the confines of their precious Council is met with instant and irrevocable fear and retribution. My beloved Brotherhood was decimated before I was seized and taken here, locked away forever, and for what?" Her face twisted, all innocence, and the first time I accepted how beautiful she was. And familiar, for some reason. How did I know that face? "For doing my best to improve the lives of all magic users."

There had to be more to it, but the likelihood I'd get anything else from her was slim to none. Which had me pondering, because there were two people in my life I could ask. One was miles away, tucked into the family's magic, Sassafras' knowledge no doubt wiped clean as was everyone else's.

The only person present who might not have been influenced by the Council's erasure coiled in fury inside me, my grandmum's echo snarling at Attica as I turned within.

Tell me, Burdie, I sent.

She didn't get to answer. Because the moment I focused within, I felt the Stronghold's power ripple and spun in surprise as the door to the staircase opened and Demetrius Strong stepped through.

With three robed figures behind him.

CHAPTER THIRTY

I might as well have not even been there, the three hurrying forward, though I recognized them instantly.

"Mistress!" The leader cast back her hood, lean face lined and scarred with old acne, eyes sunken in her face. Yes, I knew her, had a clear memory of her from the night I arrived at Coven Hall. I'd encountered these very souls in the diner outside the Yard. I knew I'd felt power, but I hadn't been able to identify it, had forgotten about it, in fact.

Encouraged to forget, and successfully? I thought them latents or some other paranormal lineage I wasn't privy to then promptly forgot them. But wait, there had been a trigger, hadn't there? Something that brushed my hand, fallen to the floor.

A book

"You left the means for someone to remember you," I said, not even realizing I said so out loud.

The woman next to me ignored me, swaying on her feet as though entranced, pausing next to me to stare at her leader. "I heard your call, mistress. I am here to serve." She fell to her knees on the stone, that same book falling to the ground before her. She appeared even more emaciated than she had yesterday, if that was possible, as though her life seeped out of her. Which, I now realized with utter horror, it was. I'd begun to feel the effects of that very power myself, in the puddle of sorcery just outside Attica's door. Had she somehow embedded her power in the book and was using it to steal the life force of the woman?

Her two companions joined her, the dark-haired man and slim boy who I'd seen at the diner so pale and empty it was obvious I was right. But before I could make any move or take action, Attica spoke.

"Thank you, my darlings." Attica's voice sounded of velvet and promises, her smile so evil I felt my skin crawl. "The time is nigh. I knew one day one of you would be strong enough to break the geas on my spell and hear my voice again."

"The guide you left blessed me with its power," the woman said, writhing on the ground in utter devotion, hands pressing to the surface of the book. "The portents of this night's arrival came so quickly, I despaired we might not succeed."

So, I was right. This date had great meaning.

"How long has it been, my children?" Attica leaned toward them, eagerness ugly on her face.

"Twenty years have come and gone," the man said. "Since you left us."

Attica hissed at that. "The geas was meant to break on the anniversary of my fall," she snarled.

"The book fell into the hands of those who had no power," the woman said. "It only came back to our Brotherhood by chance. And I was the fortunate one to find it."

I felt my heart crumble inside me. "That's how you reached me," I said, though Attica ignored me yet. It was, though. That power I'd felt released, when I'd handed it, the tingle of it. The moment Attica connected with me, though I knew it not.

Demetrius had joined me, stared at me in shock, pulling me aside. I tried to block him, to go to the trio and pull them out of harm's way. But it was far too late for that. The small family, Brotherhood all, stepped into the puddle of Attica's sorcery without encouragement. Did they know what they went to? I inhaled to warn them, but far too late.

She cackled as she pounced, and there was nothing I could do to stop her, not as the coils of power she'd managed to shove past the wards trapping her here reached up instantly and wound around the three.

And sucked the life out of them right in front of me.

Hold her! I shouted that to the Stronghold, knowing there was nothing I could do.

Even as Attica's power surged and snapped the wards keeping her bound, the recoil of blue fire— Enforcer magic left behind to guard and tend her— crackled into a ball of flame that burned out in a rush that sent agony through me.

Demetrius fell to his knees at my side, his own pain linking us through our mutual sorcery and ties to the Enforcer order. It was as though my entire body was being consumed by those same flames that welcomed me, the broken wards now distorted and tainted, searing their way through me on their way to my heart.

While Attica strode out through the now unguarded bars of her prison, the metal melting and the power of that crumbling element rushing to join itself to her own.

"How delicious," she said, laughing as she looked down at us both, blackness reaching out to devour my friend. I knew if her sorcery was allowed to touch him, Demetrius would end up like the husks of people lying on the stone, dead and turning to dust before my eyes.

"You will not." I lashed out with my own power, not sure what effect I might have but not thinking, not really.

I didn't have to. I wasn't alone, not as I feared. Burdie was with me and while I had no idea what to do with the magic that I'd just begun to know she had more than enough experience for the both of us. I felt her echo rise, the sorcery inside me answering her call, and cried out as she spun a vortex of blackness to engulf Attica, choking the woman's power even as she'd drained those she'd summoned after all this time to free her with their lives.

Attica fought, but it was obvious to me Burdie was the more skilled of the two and I was certain then and there we'd won the day, that this attempt at an escape would turn around and I could leave that despicable woman in the cell she'd been condemned to for that forever intended her.

I gave her too much credit, however, thinking

she might stand and fight. Instead, howling in fury, she pushed back with one last surge of her own power and ran.

While slamming her magic into Demetrius so hard he fell backward.

Of course, I hesitated. Burdie did, too, her mental voice crying out, *Jack!* Memory flared, images I didn't recognize, a handsome young man I didn't know reaching toward me, toward my grandmum, a golden hand extended that caught the light in my mind's eye. I blinked, frozen in place, Burdie screaming in fury while Thaddea prodded me to move, to do something.

Too late again, time gone in a place that held no time in it, because when I finally did jerk free of the memory Burdie found herself lost in, the door to the staircase had thudded shut and the worse had happened.

Attica Brindle escaped. But not without one last gift.

You asked, she sent, cackling in my mind. *I answer.*

I was already stumbling toward the stairs, going after her, when it hit me all at once. The truth, her past, her history, that same history once erased now mine to bear as she bore it. And the truth of it brought me to my knees.

Children scream in agony as sorcery devours them from the inside, their witch magic unable to protect them from the disease of artificial implantation. While Attica and her people try over and over again to implant that power in those unprepared for it. Because it was obvious to me as I sank further and further into the unmistakable core of the matter, that every soul carried the seed of sorcery. But this method, and the madness that was Attica Brindle and her plan, pushed that blossom of darkness from the gentle and dormant magic I knew into a ravening monster fit on consuming everything in its path until the host died in agony.

And now you know, she sent. *I can't wait to try again.*

Burdie wasn't the only one screaming her name. I found myself stumbling after her, Demetrius calling for me as he pursued me, the Stronghold silent in the vaults of my mind. Why had it let her go? I raged at myself, at Attica, at the ineffectuality of my interference, though if Demetrius had gone alone, as I now know he would have managed thanks to me, he would have died with that family.

This was not the time to reassure myself, but for action, for fury. I don't remember my descent, nor my race through the halls of the Stronghold, out the portal and into the cool September air of the Yard, bursting into the world I knew with Attica's sorcery my only guide, even as I reached, with command I wasn't expecting, for the last person I ever expected to speak to again.

MAHALIA. She connected immediately, if sullenly, my mother's magic locking onto me.

You'd better have a good—

I slammed against her with Attica's face and the truth she'd shared with me, feeling the family magic, the Hayle coven's power, waken and shake her as firmly as I had.

You have her inside you, too, I sent. *GrandMum Burdie. Ask her. ASK HER.*

To my surprise, she did. Then roared, *COME WITH ME.*

I felt her surge into me, trying to take me over, but I fought her off, retaining control, though I fully accepted her offer of magic. I had only a fraction of Burdie's magic and her echo with me. My mother had all of the memories, all of the history, at her disposal and clearly took that witch's reaction seriously. She might not have had the full story, but for whatever reason that was her own, Mahalia Hayle reacted as I needed her to for once.

We passed the wards of the Yard long before I could remember leaving Harvard might trigger the kind of response that would end my time here.

Nothing mattered, not my Enforcer power, not the sorcerer I knew followed me with panic in his mind, and certainly not what Headmistress Kirstin Lund might think of me.

I'd let a monster loose, for better or worse, and I couldn't let that stand.

I caught up with Attica three blocks from the Yard, though it was quickly apparent she'd stopped to wait for me. The Brotherhood leader waved from the corner of the street, the light above her draining slowly as she sucked its power inside her, arms rising as she exulted in the experience.

"So much magic," she said. "So much more available now than ever before." I watched her power grow and knew if I didn't act now, I'd never get the chance.

She'd eat the whole world.

This way. Burdie had taken control of my mother, as well, and did the same through me, linking to the echo I carried, deep thrum of sorcery rising in a wave from me. I felt my being split, as though the black power carved a way between the witch and Fey, surging forward to engulf Attica. For one brief moment I feared she might siphon off what the echo used against her, only to realize the Brotherhood leader's mistake even as Burdie engulfed her in darkness tied to a humming golden power that felt like infinity and cold, logical control.

Now, Burdie sent.

Together for the first time ever, Hayle witches all, we drew out every scrap of magic our enemy had in her possession in one giant gulp.

It was over as fast as it began, the wave retreating to me, snapping back into place, soft burp of satisfaction vibrating through me while Attica stared, pale and shaking and frozen in place.

She started to scream and didn't stop, shrieking as she stared at her hands, shaking them in my direction. I stumbled toward her, still divided, my mother continuing to fight me for dominance even as Burdie did the same, the three of us battling harder than the stripping of Attica had required.

"Ethpeal!" I was physically spun around, Ivan standing over me, Demetrius panting at his side, Varity with them, trembling as she tugged me away from the Dumont Enforcer trainee and hugged me tight.

I struggled for release as I registered the silence in the street, turning to find Attica had vanished into the night. My power lashed out, my mother seeking while Burdie lashed a whip of sorcery out into the darkness but they both relented a moment later.

There was nothing to find, to sense. Attica Brindle had escaped but she had done so powerless.

So be it, Burdie whispered. *My love to you, daughter of my heart.* I was surprised by that address, the coherence of her voice often subjective rather than so clearly spoken. Though even more so when I realized it wasn't aimed at my mother. Because a moment later her echo slapped Mahalia hard inside the confines of my mind. *Traitor*, the part of my grandmum that remained with my mother said before retreating back into the family magic.

Which left me alone with my mother. No, not quite. The powers of Burdie and Thaddea stood with me, my sorcery blossoming beneath, Fey magic that was a gift from my father burning green and rumbling like a coming storm of my own. And the magic, the witch magic I bore, offered a warning to Mahalia. It would not forget the family magic was once meant to be mine.

And it would not let her forget, either.

My mother didn't say a word, sliding away from me with what felt like real shame and hatred that burned as bright as the Enforcer fire.

Good riddance, Burdie whispered.

I couldn't agree more.

CHAPTER THIRTY-ONE

I stood in Headmistress Lund's office with dread in my heart but unable to muster a defense. Not that I needed one as the people around me argued so loudly I could barely make out their individual voices as the shouting grew to a cacophony that smothered me in sound and deafened me with pressure.

It was hard to focus on my future at the moment, after what I'd just been through, so whatever Lund's decision, I would live with it. I was more curious, to be honest, about the golden power my grandmum let me feel, terrified of it as I was excited by it, and by the amazing volume of magic I'd absorbed from Attica, as yet unexplored.

My skin crawled a little at the idea of that stolen energy's origins, but the blossom of darkness didn't seem the least bit squeamish.

"ENOUGH!" Gordon's voice cut through everyone else. I winced a little, if only because she interrupted my thoughts, noting that several of the Council members—yes, they were all present, some in their dressing gowns and not appearing happy about the fact—had clumped together and were glaring in my direction. They were in Lund's camp, no doubt, and would be voting against me when it came down to it.

"Council Leader Gordon," Lund said smoothly as if she hadn't just been yelling herself five seconds ago. "Surely, the time has come to finally rid ourselves once and for all of the poison that is the Hayle bloodline."

Gordon fixed her with such wrath that Lund couldn't meet her eyes for long. "Did you just suggest we execute a student, Kirstin?"

The Headmistress blanched. "I didn't mean..." she fumbled for words, spluttering. Well, at least she didn't want me dead, so there was that small miracle. No, she wanted me alive to suffer and to live with the fact I would never be an Enforcer or a member of a coven ever again and I would live out my life alone and lost in the normal world.

I realized then and there, while I knew I would

survive such a fate easily, I would rather they followed through and took my life after all. I was an Enforcer and if I couldn't be, I chose death.

The Enforcer fire flared inside me as if protesting any chance of it leaving, so I took that as comfort, though I had no doubt when the time came—any second now—Noe-Bradford was ordered to take it from me it would have to obey her.

"Council Leader," Demetrius spoke up, clear voice ringing, "none of this is on Ethpeal. I asked her to help me. If anyone should face the blame, it's me."

We'd taken turns filling everyone assembled in on what had happened after Lund's insistence anyone of any kind of authority come to her office and witness my downfall. That meant not only were Gilleland and Carista present for my shaming, so was the recently returned Enforcer Leader Raoul Donovan who seemed unable to do much but scowl at everyone and mutter to himself.

"No," Lisa Noe-Bradford interrupted, cutting Demetrius off. "This was my responsibility." She took a step between me and Lund, and I wasn't surprised to find Gilleland and Carista joined her, though what good it would do I had no idea.

"If you're all done throwing yourselves in the

line of fire," Gordon said with some sarcasm.

"Council Leader," Gilleland began.

"I said enough," she snapped, "and I meant it. Step back, please."

The trio did, if reluctantly, though I was grateful for their attempt to protect me. Knowing what was inevitable, I took one stride forward myself, head high, shoulders back.

"I will accept whatever is to come," I said, "but know that Attica Brindle is still at large, and I will pursue her until I find her and bring her back to justice or I die trying."

Lund snorted, looking around for support for her derision, though even the Council members who supported her no longer seemed fully on her side. It appeared that by taking her power, Burdie had broken the long-standing spell and freed the history of the Brotherhood's leader to the world again. I knew from their expressions each of them had at least partial knowledge of what she'd done, Vespa Rhodes the palest of them all as the historian for the Council.

"It is not Ethpeal's fault this evil creature escaped justice," she said, voice shaking. "It is our arrogance as a Council. She should have been stripped and executed twenty years ago. Instead, we chose to enact a foolish plan of vengeance against her and only laid the groundwork for our own downfall. Arrogant." She shook her head, shoulders bowing. "I am ashamed of us and will remain so all the rest of my days."

"I for one had nothing to do with it." Why wasn't I surprised when Chloe Dumont refused to accept any responsibility? I caught Odette standing behind Lund, her flicker of attitude matching her aunt's, the Council member's faintly French accent cutting instead of softening. "I refuse to take responsibility for something our predecessors did."

"Blame is irrelevant at this juncture," Gordon said, the others muttering before falling quiet. "I was Council Leader when Attica Brindle was sentenced. I take responsibility. There, are you happy now, Chloe?"

The Dumont member shrugged. "Perhaps this should be discussed among the Council," she said. "And your role reassessed over this matter."

I wasn't the only one who gasped, I can tell you that, though Gordon took the blatant challenge in stride.

"We shall indeed do so," Gordon said, crips and confident. "Though if you think you can do my job, I wish you the best in it."

Chloe couldn't seem to hold Gordon's gaze and finally looked away while my insides churned in worry for my great-grandmother's friend. She'd done so much for me, risked so much. Was I about to cost her the position she'd held all these years?

This is not on you, she sent to me in a tight bit of magic, clearly knowing where my mind had taken me. Not for a moment. *Well done, Ethpeal, for your part in this. I am, and will always be, very proud of you. Your mother is a fool.*

I WILL BE HEARD. As though Gordon's words summoned her, that very witch chose her moment well, and I realized only then she'd been with me all along. Of course, she had, watching and waiting and likely laughing at all of us through the geas she'd laid upon me. Had she known all along where I'd end up? Or merely wanted her revenge for my years of not fulfilling the role she'd planned for me. Whatever the case, Mahalia Hayle appeared in her own wash of magical fire not unlike the Enforcer power that clung to its hold on me, her image solidifying until she appeared so real, I was certain if I reached out to touch her I'd make contact with her skin.

She was still as beautiful as ever, though even I could see, with this bit of distance, just how big a toll the family magic's resistance was taking on her. The fact she'd stripped my grandmother, Lilibeth, before the coven's power was ready to leave that witch for my mother had meant a constant struggle between the coven's leader and the very core of power that sustained our family. Yes, our family. I was and always would be a Hayle, for better or worse.

Whatever the case, however, the coven magic seemed eager enough to support her in this instance, and I hoped it had to do with the family itself reaching out to me.

"You are not welcome here." Lund was practically shaking with rage. "Get out of my office, demon spawn."

"I will be heard." My mother smiled at her, wiggling her fingers in Lund's direction. "Dear Kirstin, how lovely to see you again. I hope the Dumonts are treating you well." Mahalia's nasty laughter cut off as she spun toward me. "Ethpeal," she said. "An Enforcer, my daughter, really? Of all the things you could be?"

"You didn't exactly give me a choice, did you?" I refused to call her mother even now. "Thank you for your final gift." I certainly didn't mean it.

She shrugged somewhat delicately, obviously enjoying herself. "You're far too valuable to be wasted on some random family who don't deserve you." She'd banished me. Made sure I'd never have another coven to call home. And she dared treat this like she'd acted with benevolence? I almost lost my temper. Would have.

But for Thaddea.

That ancestress forced my lips into a gentle smile. "If you say so," she said. "Maleah." Why would she call my mother that? *Because that was what I called her*, Thaddea sent. *And she needs to know you are not alone.*

I'd never seen my mother blanch before. Registered the understanding in her eyes, the sudden flare of rage that followed. Now she knew it wasn't just Burdie I carried, but Thaddea as well and the realization almost set her off. Probably would have if we'd been alone or in less prominent company. I watched her pull herself together visibly, her fury I'd somehow retained parts of the two women who'd done their best to raise her when her own mother failed so terribly, had to be eating her alive.

And could be the only reason she said what she did next.

"I repeal Ethpeal's banishment." She did *what*? I lurched, the family magic rippling around her, though her herculean effort kept it from vacating her immediately and coming to me. As it was, a tiny scrap won free—or was let loose—and slammed into me, huddling inside me, joining my two ancestresses as it coiled around them and shuddered at its return. "She is again a full member of the Hayle family, if the least of us." Oh, she loved that idea, the woman who bore me. She jerked tight on the reins and the coven's power fell in line, if sullenly, while I gaped at my mother. "And as a Hayle member, in absentia, I believe all this nonsense about her not being welcome at Coven Hall is dealt with." She spun on Lund who looked about ready to lose her mind. "Correct?"

"Correct!" Vespa Rhodes nodded decisively.

And while it was utterly obvious to me Mahalia was only acting out of spite and hatefulness, she had no idea she'd just given me exactly what I wanted.

A place to belong.

"Thank you, Mother," I said spitefully and with a smile while hers faded.

"Study hard, dear," she shot back. And vanished.

CHAPTER THIRTY-TWO

I walked the halls of the Stronghold, Enforcer power simmering inside me, still burning from my first training session and my initial encounter with the Enforcer Leader. He hadn't held back, buffeting me soundly with his own magic, only to retreat after a short period and a shake of his head.

"Welcome to the order, Ethpeal Hayle," Raoul Donovan said, as though I'd needed his acceptance when the blue flames engulfed me in their joy.

It had been an odd two days, waffling between worry about Attica (who I'd been forbidden from pursuing on pain of death by Di Gordon) and her plans despite her lack of power and excitement over the fact I might actually get to have what I wanted after all. There had been so many ups and downs in such a short space of time it took those two days before class began for me to shake off the pall of anxiety that lingered, and even now I felt its fingers prodding my mind, seeking a place to sneak inside and give me trouble.

I wouldn't allow it. Whatever came from this moment forward, I would work hard, study hard (with no intent to please my mother, however) and be the best Enforcer I could ever be.

My friends had come to me as soon as the meeting wrapped up, Varity's embrace, Deloras' shaking cheek kiss, Demetrius' bear hug and even Jeffery's tight squeeze all forcing me to the brink of tears. But it was Ivan stepping away from Odette, pulling his arm roughly from her hand, that Dumont staring after him with hurt and rage on her face while he joined us to take his turn hugging me that made me laugh instead of cry.

I made enemies, of course, I had, but my friends were far more numerous.

As for the Council, I was happy to hear over tea with Gordon just that morning any challenge against her had been quashed.

"I'll keep my place for now," she told me, patting my hand with a sad smile while I let relief win at last. "But perhaps it is nearing the time my successor has her chance to shine. I am reminded, my dear, that younger powers should have the chance to prevail and that my family has waited a long time for me to come home."

I'd forgotten she was a Bradford, that when her time was done, she could retire in peace and quiet back in the embrace of her family's magic. But I really hoped that time would come a long time in the future.

I ran both hands down the front of my velvet robe, a birthday gift from my wonderful advocate, smiling at the memory of her bright eyes as she handed it to me.

"You already make me proud," she'd said.

Both of my mentors in my regular studies in Coven Hall had joined in the hugging brigade, Kate Carista squealing when I walked through the entry to the main hall earlier this morning, David Gilleland beaming and whispering he was proud of me before handing me a giant stack of scrolls and books and assuring me I had a great deal of work to do.

Work that waited for my attention back in my room. I'd get to it. But I had something to do first.

I'd peeked into the circular chamber at the base of the tower, now open and fully examined by Noe-Bradford and Leader Donovan. It had been sealed off from their knowledge, their surprise even the Stronghold had forgotten about it ending in both

Enforcers reclaiming the space for the purpose it had been intended. Though I hoped that it would be a very long time before anyone of any sufficient power requiring that space as their prison showed their face again.

All of my requests to my grandmum about her history with the Brotherhood were ignored. In fact, it seemed as though Burdie had retreated far inside me and refused to come out at all. Whatever had happened, it carried obvious trauma and left scars behind her echo wasn't willing to face. When I tried to talk to Thaddea, she just felt sad and turned away, too.

Honestly, if it hadn't been for my present circumstances, I wouldn't have felt more alone in my life. Fortunately, I had a new family to fill the void, though I had no idea just how much I missed my two ancestresses and their steady presences until they cut themselves off from me.

Speaking of which, Demetrius had been avoiding me as well, though he claimed it wasn't personal. His promise to teach me what I needed to know about sorcery had fallen to the wayside, leaving me to fumble along on my own. That left space for Ivan, naturally, and though I wished otherwise, the tall Dumont had proven himself trustworthy and took great effort to show affection and attention. Not that I needed either. I wanted my friend back, the connection of sorcery something I missed. Whatever Demetrius was up to, he wanted me out of it.

We'd just see about that.

I paused at the entry to the meeting hall, knowing what was coming despite the fact my friends did their best to surprise me. Hard to do when the very stones whispered to me and didn't know that revealing what was coming might not be the best choice.

They seem excited, the Stronghold sent.

It's my birthday, I sent back.

I see. It paused. *I never understood your kind's purpose of tracking years. Is it that important to you?*

I laughed and stepped through the door, triggering the thin ward set across it. Light burst overhead, the collective waiting for me on the other side shouting out in glee, "Happy birthday, Ethpeal!"

Ah, the Stronghold sent as Varity latched onto me, laughing and squeezing so hard I could barely breathe while not minding the hug one bit. *I understand. Happy birthday, Enforcer Hayle, Leader Hayle, Steam Union Sorcerer Hayle.*

Thank you, I sent, not sure what any of that meant but grateful, nonetheless. *It really is.*

WHAT'S NEXT?

Found yourself with Ethpeal but no idea who the Hayles are? Looking for more? There's so much available for you in this universe!

From the **Hayle Coven Novels** to the **Blood and Gold Trilogy** (Burdie Hayle's first adventure!) and many more, get lost in the magic of the Hayle Coven and happy reading!

Find the full series available now at all retailers!

Family Magic
Witch Hunt
Demon Child
The Wild
The Long Lost
Gatekeeper
Flesh and Blood
Full Circle
Divided Heart
First Plane
Light and Shadow
Queen of Darkness
Dark Promise
Unseelie Ties
Ancient Ways
The Undying
Shifting Loyalties
Enforcer
Coven Leader
The Last Call

Welcome to the family!

ABOUT THE AUTHOR

EVERYTHING YOU NEED TO know about me is in this one statement: I've wanted to be a writer since I was a little girl, and now I'm doing it. How cool is that, being able to follow your dream and make it reality? I've tried everything from university to college, graduating the second with a journalism diploma (I sucked at telling real stories), am an enthusiastic member of an all-girl improv troupe (if you've never tried it, I highly recommend making things up as you go along as often as possible) and I get to teach and perform with an amazing group of women I adore. I've even been in a Celtic girl band (some of our stuff is on YouTube!) and was an independent filmmaker. My life has been one creative thing after another—all leading me here, to writing books for a living.

Now with multiple series in happy publication, I live on beautiful and magical Prince Edward Island (I know you've heard of Anne of Green Gables) with my multitude of pets.

I love-love-love hearing from you! You can reach me (and I promise I'll message back) at patti@pattilarsen.com. And if you're eager for your next dose of Patti Larsen books (usually about one release a month) come join my mailing list! All the best up and coming, giveaways, contests and, of course, my observations on the world (aren't you just dying to know what I think about everything?) all in one place: http://bit.ly/PattiLarsenEmail.

Last—but not least!—I hope you enjoyed what you read! Your happiness is my happiness. And I'd love to hear just what you thought. A review where you found this book would mean the world to me—reviews feed writers more than you will ever know. So, loved it (or not so much), your honest review would make my day. Thank you!